I0451315

WARREN

PERRY'S NEST BOOK 2

KATHI S. BARTON

This is a work of fiction. Names, characters, places, and incidents are products of the author's imagination or are used fictitiously and are not to be construed as real. Any resemblance to actual events, locations, organizations, or persons, living or dead, is entirely coincidental.

World Castle Publishing, LLC
Pensacola, Florida
Copyright © Kathi S. Barton 2022
Hardback ISBN: 9798370537059
Paperback ISBN: 9781960076120
eBook ISBN: 9781960076137
First Edition World Castle Publishing, LLC, December 21, 2022
http://www.worldcastlepublishing.com
Licensing Notes
All rights reserved. No part of this book may be used or reproduced in any manner whatsoever without written permission, except in the case of brief quotations embodied in articles and reviews.
Cover: Karen Fuller
Editor: Karen Fuller

Prologue

Warren wandered around the rooms he'd been given while staying with Hamish and Lander. It was a great room. Not at all feminine like he'd expected when Hamish told him Lander had decorated it for him especially. The bathroom was done up well, with lots of warm colors like the bedroom had. The windows in here, like the bedroom, were covered in room-darkening curtains that made it so he could rest during the day if he wished.

He hadn't packed much. A laptop, some books he'd been reading, as well as some paperwork he'd not gotten finished while he'd been at home. Smiling to himself as he left the rooms, Warren wondered what his buddy would think about him owning a blood bank. Not for himself—no, feeding for himself had never been a problem—but for hospitals and other medical facilities that had a need for rare or even not so rare blood.

Lander, he assumed it was her, was coming up the stairs as he was going toward them. When she got to the top of them, she put out her hand in greeting. Taking it, something with the touch of their hands blew them both backward and to the floor. His last thought before he hit his head and passed out was that Hamish was going to kill him if he hurt his mate.

When he woke, he was lying on his bed. Sitting up quickly, not sure what was going on, he was told to lie back down by Hamish. He did as he'd been told because he wasn't sure how much longer he'd have been able to stay in that position. Hamish asked him if he was all right.

"Never mind that. Is your mate all right?" He just grinned. "I'm assuming since I'm still alive that I didn't hurt her enough for you to want to kill me."

"She had a nasty bump on her head, but it,

like yours, has healed. Lander is resting right now. Not because of the power exchange, but because she is newly turned and needs to rest during the day." Warren decided he was feeling well enough to sit up now and cautiously did so. Feeling better, he moved to the chair beside Hamish. "Lander told me that all she did was touch your hand in greeting, and the two of you were blasted by something. I don't know what you got, but she has a great deal more power on some things than I do. Can you feel any differences?"

"Not yet. My mind is still processing the fact that a new vampire blasted me across the hall." They both laughed. "I honestly don't know what happened. Did she give anything to me? Am I the one that blasted us apart? Right now, I'm just grateful she wasn't hurt."

"As am I. However, you'll be happy to know she told me that if I touched you with harm in my mind, she'd break off my fangs and stab me with them. Lander's used that one before. Every time she threatens me with it, I get more afraid. She's a pistol, as Grandda says." Again they both laughed. Warren got up to stretch. Then before he could put his arms down from the most wonderful stretch he'd had, he paused. "You figured something out?"

"Yes. Lander isn't sleeping right now but coming down the hall toward us. Your grandda is on a construction site on the other side of town, giving the men working a break by telling them stories. He knew they needed to step back a moment. Something about the homeowner changing their mind several times a day about the house. A woman, I'm sure is your sister, is on her computer, looking at her financial records. She's about broke, so you might want to talk to her about it. Colleen is being extorted by someone in Virginia about her being a vampire. Their last name is Pfizer. She's paying them hush money, she calls it, so you'll not find out." Warren turned to his best friend. "I've never been able to do that before. Especially with your sister, whom I've never met. Lander is coming into the room now."

The door opened, and there was Lander. She was staring at him like she was trying to gauge him on some level. Warren asked her what she'd gotten from him, knowing that was why she was here. He also realized at that moment that he couldn't read her mind. That scared him more than anything else.

"When I touch something, something as mundane as a hairbrush, I can tell not only where it's been, who the owner is, but what the person died from. I've never used the brush set that was laid out, but I know now that it belonged to Hamish's grandmother, and she was killed by a human who had not meant to kill her. They'd been friends." Lander shivered when she put her hand on the chair he'd been sitting in. "I want to toss this chair out as soon as possible. It has been used for obscene things that I don't care to discuss."

Hamish touched his finger to the chair, and it disappeared.

Just like that, he did his mate's bidding. And better yet, he believed her when she said it had to go. Sitting on the edge of the bed, his chair now gone, Warren stood up quickly because he didn't want to think about what had happened on the mattress.

"You're the only one other than the delivery

people who have touched it. If it makes you feel any better, it was sealed up when it arrived, and Hamish used his magic to put it here in this room." He told her it did. "I can find people. What I mean is I can sense where they are and what they're doing. I can also tell that you can do the same. Have you touched anything in here?"

"I sat in the chair that is now gone." She asked him to touch something in the room. Then she suggested the framed art on the wall. Warren did so without hesitation. "No. I don't feel anything other than I can see that it's been cleaned recently. Could that be it?"

Warren touched several more things in the room without any kind of feelings from it. When he asked if they could leave the room, the three of them did so without saying a word. Entering the living room, he wanted to just think for a minute. Let his mind wrap around what he was feeling at the moment.

"I came here to say my goodbyes to you, Hamish. I had it in my head that I was too old and lonely to live out my days as a hermit. Then I get blasted across the hall by a pretty woman, and I feel revived. Like? Well, like I've been given a purpose again. I don't know what that is, but I do feel that way." Hamish told him he was happy for them all then. "Yes, so am I. This thing, finding people, I've only just realized that while I know what they're doing and where they are, I can't read their emotions with it. It's like I've been given some information, and what I do with it is up to me. Does that make sense?"

"Yes. When I find bodies or cars, whatever I'm looking at, I can feel the last few minutes of their lives. Like the man I found just a few days ago. I knew he thought he was pulling into a parking lot to enjoy his ice cream before it melted. When he hit the water, he had no fear because he didn't equate where he was with dying. I knew that he enjoyed his few bites of ice cream before he hit the water, but I only know that because I could see it in his mind. Not the emotions he'd have while enjoying it."

Warren changed the subject about what had

happened and told the couple what else he'd been doing. Closing down some of his businesses was one of the things he'd thought he'd regret now that he had a better outlook on life. But he didn't, he told them.

"I can start fresh. Try new things. Honestly, it's been a long time since I've wanted to do anything more than just go from day to day." Lander asked him if he suffered from depression. "I believe that for all single vampires, as well as any creature that has lived as long as Hamish and I, depression is a constant battle. With me losing my mate, too, that didn't help. She was, much like you are to Hamish, my world. I miss her less and less, but my heart still grieves for what I have lost."

"I'm so sorry about that. But I am happy you're here with us now and that you will be for a long time. You will, correct?" He said he would, but he couldn't live with them. "And why the hell not? It's not like we don't have plenty of room here."

"I think he's telling us he needs his own space, love. Not that he doesn't want to hang out with us.

As a single vampire, he'll need space." She didn't seem to understand but let it go. Hamish winked at him. "I actually have a home you might like. It's not far from here. And you'll just take it because you told me about my sister."

"What's happening with Colleen?" Hamish told her, and Warren filled in the details as he got them. "What are we going to do about it then? I'm sure you've been thinking up a plan."

"I have. But I'm going to talk to Colleen first. Details will be important in this kind of situation, as this person might have more details than he's telling my sister. Or, he might not have anything at all and has targeted her for some reason." Lander said he had to die. "Yes, well, how about we table that one for now and wait on details?"

"Yes, all right. But we're going to help her, right? I love her as much as you do, and I don't want her stressed." Warren loved the little spit-fire woman. When she turned to him with a smile, he felt his beast hiding in the shadows as if he were afraid of her. "You, my dear friend, are going to help me out with a few projects I have going on in my head. But first and foremost, I need answers to a great many questions. I've been reading the book that Hamish's grandma had, but there are things in there that I can do that aren't mentioned for a newbie. Do you guys really call newly made vampires a newbie?"

"Honey, no offense, but I think an entire book could be written about you and being newly changed. And if being called a newbie is something that bothers you? Then I shall promise on my deceased wife's heart that I'll never call anyone that again."

The rest of the afternoon into the evening was spent talking about anything and everything. When Lander got a phone call, she left the room to go answer it. He'd never bothered with a cell phone before as if anyone had wanted to contact him, and they'd not met before that, he wasn't in the mood to talk to them. But now — well, he wasn't so sure about a lot of things anymore.

The one thought that kept going around and around in his head was just how strong Hamish was that he could turn a human into one of their kind, and she have such amazing powers? Was he a leader? If not, he surely would make a good one. No one would mess with him once they met his mate. Christ, she was amazing.

~*~

Warren liked the old building that he thought would make a good shop for him. Long ago, he'd been a jewelry maker. The level of concentration kept his mind occupied and not thinking about things that were better not thought of at all. He pulled out his cell phone, a new addition to his life, and called the number on the "for rent" sign hanging in the window. He burst out laughing when he contacted Hamish.

"Do you own everything around here?" Hamish told him about the building he was looking at. "What have you done for improvements then? To me, it looks like it could have been built yesterday but still has its old-time charm."

"I had the stained glassed windows throughout the house repaired. There are also transom windows of stained glass on both floors. The furnace is new, and so is the roof. It had been slate, but I sold it all off in trade for the tin roof it has now. I guess the installer's wife is into crafty things." Hamish asked him if he wanted it. "I'll give it to you just to get it off my back. I've owned it for some time, and since things have been bad around here for a while, no one has the funds to rent it."

"I can't just take it from you." Hamish asked him why not. "I'm not sure. I just don't want you to give me a house because you're tired of paying taxes on it. That's it, isn't it?"

"Some of it. However, it's a nice place inside and out. There is ample parking in the back for whatever you want to do with it. What do you want to do with it?" He told him what he'd been thinking about doing. "In the basement, which is super nice with walls and cable hookups, there are two tables that I can only assume were built in the place. Then someone concreted them to the floor. Sturdy as fuck. And the tops of both of them are steel and have electrical outlets all around them."

"How do I get in?" He told him he was in town

and would meet him there in a few minutes. "Is Lander with you? I was worried about her all night last night."

"She is with me and feeling better today. We've been scouting out buildings she can use for her dad's legacy." The car pulled into the back lot, and Warren went around to meet them. Lander did look better today. "We've found three buildings we are thinking of using. The one we'll more than likely use is the one just outside of town. That way, the city won't have too much to bitch about when we're having things delivered."

"I've been looking for blankets and things for a kit for people in transit, with things like deodorants and shaving kits. Soap too." Warren told Lander if she needed help packing them up, he'd gladly help. "Thank you. I might take you up on that. Also, I'm looking for a doctor and a psychiatrist. If you know of anyone that would be on board with this project, let me know. I know you were a doctor at some time in your life, Hamish told me, but I'm not hinting that you should do it. I don't want anyone helping unless they're doing it because they want to and not because they think they have to. Does that make sense?"

"Yes. And I know of a psychiatrist that might be willing to come here. He's not a vampire but a bear shifter. His name is Calhoun Meyer. There is also a human that might work out for you by the name of Brad Kirk. Nice man. He's an ancient that has been around for more than five hundred years. Someone gifted him immortality for saving a life. If he has more magic than that, I don't know what it might be." Lander kissed him on the cheek. "Not that I don't mind, but what was that for?"

"For not telling me you'd do it when I know you want this building for something else altogether. Good for you. I love you, Warren." He was embarrassed. Rather than digging himself in deeper with his embarrassment, he told her what his plans were. "Now, let's go see about getting this home in your name so you can make beautiful jewelry that will be on every beautiful woman in the world."

When she walked off and opened the door to the building, Warren looked at Hamish. He didn't look pissy because his mate had kissed him. More like he was resigned to the fact that she was going to do it no matter what he asked her not to do. Warren wondered if he'd asked her not to touch other males. He decided he really didn't want to know.

"You'll take the building if for no other reason than I need you to. Not for the taxes, but because you've made Lander so happy about this. Helping you." Warren told him he'd make the first piece of jewelry for her. "You do that, and she'll be sobbing about how lovely it is and who gave it to her."

They both laughed and entered the large building. The first thing he saw was the stained glass window at the side of the building in what appeared to be a parlor. The fireplace in there was marble, something he had in his home in Spain. He was already in love with the place.

The tour of the house was fun. Lander told him what he should use the extra rooms for on the main floor. It looked to him like someone had added another wing on the house that was one floor. It appeared to have been used as a large walk-in pantry. He told her he was going to use it as a darkroom so he could rest safely during the hottest part of the day.

"Brilliant. I have rooms like that now too. Only we used darkening curtains. It's amazing to me how much light they cut out and still look pretty in a room."

She and Hamish went to the kitchen to let him go to the basement. He knew he'd rarely use the kitchen area, but he was going to have it updated. Appearances were everything when you didn't trust humans all that much.

The tables that Hamish had told him about were perfect in every way for what he'd use them for. One of them was waist level so he could sit while using it. The other was about four feet from the floor and the perfect height for him to stand up and work on. He was also happy to see that the plugs on the table were ones that could take machinery plugged into them and not have a problem.

He unearthed a kiln at the corner of the building outdoors. At some point in his life, he'd been a potter as well. This kiln, used for raku firings, was going to come in handy for other projects he had in mind.

Warren found boxes of clay that weren't dried out, as well as an entire shelf of glazes in the basement. His creative juices were flowing now, and he wanted to rush the couple off so he could have some fun.

Just as he was headed up the open stairs, he saw something under them. Going back there, being careful of what it might be, he found a safe.

Calling down Hamish and Lander, he showed them what he'd found, then asked Hamish if he'd noticed it before. After telling him no, but it looked as if it had been there for some time, they moved all the debris off and around it. They all agreed it hadn't just been put in. When Lander put her hand on the six by at least ten safe, she smiled at him.

"The combination is twelve right, twenty-five left, and sixteen right." Shaking his head, he opened the safe on the first try. Inside of it was not just the combination but a list of things that had been put in it and taken out with the dates. "It looks like the dates on some of those things are a couple hundred years old. I wonder why he did that."

"Could be that he was keeping track of things so he'd not think something was missing. If he took it out and wrote it down, then when he came back to it, he'd know it wasn't supposed to be in there. Same with the things he put in here." Warren pulled out the first leather sack and laid it on the floor. "If you'd be so kind as to open this for me because you made it so easy for me to get into."

Lander dumped the bag onto the shorter table. He was glad he'd sat down in one of the chairs that had been around the table, or he might well have fallen. Touching his finger to the large diamond, he couldn't believe what a find this was. Hamish pulled the other nine bags out and dumped them on the table in separate piles.

There were yellow diamonds, blue ones, as well as sapphires, opals, and rubies. Two bags of emeralds that were unpolished like the rest of them were. The last bag held an assortment of stones. Tiger's eye, some little pebbles that had been polished to a high sheen that showed the colors off brilliantly.

"I can't take this. The house belongs to you,

Hamish. Surely you know this is worth millions." Lander picked up the tiger's eye stone and held it tightly in her hand while Hamish said it was Warren's. "No. I won't accept this. It's entirely too much. You have to take these bags of gems, or we don't have a deal on any of it."

"The man that put these in here had a lovely little shop in the parlor of this house. He would work nightly on things and go to work in the morning to go to estate sales, household sales, and such. Most of the time, these items were in jewelry boxes that had a great deal of junk gems mixed in with it. His name was Clarence Brown. I think you've heard of him?" Warren and Hamish both nodded. "He made a living going to different places, and since he never spent anything more than a few dollars for things, he was never thought of as a man who had millions of dollars' worth of gems in his workshop."

"He died some time ago. I remember reading about it in the newspaper, saying how he'd died a pauper. Little did anyone know he was a millionaire several times over." Lander told him that was right.

"So none of this is stolen? He paid for it all?"

"Oh yes. There were times he thought of it as stolen goods for as little as he paid for it. However, he used the cash he'd made from his jewelry, which was the reason they thought him broke, to put food on the table of a great many people without them ever knowing who it was that helped them. Mr. Brown had no children—his wife died when they were newly married. He had no one to carry on his work, and I find that the saddest story I've ever heard. So if you don't take these gems and stones and carry on the things that this man did, then I'm going to have to hurt you. You know I can, Warren. This man gave his all to help others. You need to do the same with the things he left for you to find."

"Lander, I love you. So much." She told Warren she dearly loved him too. "All right. I'll do it. But you have to pick out a stone so I can make you something beautiful for your help." She handed him the tiger's eye, telling him what she wanted. "It would be a lovely necklace, but it wouldn't be worthy of you, I'm afraid."

"That was the first stone he found. The first one he polished. Not by machine but with his hands and tools. I want you to make me a necklace fitting of the man who took the time to do that. Please?"

He nodded. Warren didn't think he'd ever get used to someone like Lander. She was the most special person he'd ever known in all his life.

As they were bagging the items up and putting them back into the bags, each one he touched, he could almost see how it would look as a piece of jewelry. Excitement raced over his skin, and he was wanting to get started. However, he needed to get some equipment out of storage and also gather up things like wires and such to make things work for him.

After doing a good search of the basement, they headed to the shed out back. There was where he found all the equipment that had been used by Mr. Brown. Most of it wasn't viable anymore, and it was covered with rust. But he did find a great deal of wire that he'd need, as well as all the polishing rags the man had worn down to nearly nothing.

"I'm going to enjoy this." Hamish told him he could tell. "I don't know what I'll do with the rest of the house, but I'm thinking it might make a good shop for high-end things. It might not sell well around here, but I'll make sure I have a good online presence too. I'm sure I have enough junk at my home that I could easily bring here with the help of you guys. Also, before I forget again to tell you." Warren laughed when he thought about what he'd done. "I purchased the candy bars the kids are selling twice yesterday and donated them back to them. I bet you guys are helping them too."

Lander told him how they were going to fly them out there and put them up in a hotel for an extra couple of days. Every kid should experience New York at least once at Christmas time. Hamish said he was going too, but as a shopper. He was taking Lander for her first visit.

"I might join you if you'd not mind." Lander told him that would be wonderful. "Maybe by then, I'll have my head out of my ass and working again. I didn't realize how much I needed this."

As they were leaving the house, a car pulled into the driveway. As soon as the woman got out of the car, he knew that this was Colleen, Hamish's sister. She looked like him enough to know they were related, but she didn't look manly. She was beautiful.

"Hello. You must be Warren. I've heard about you all my life." He put out his hand to shake hers. "My goodness, you're handsome, aren't you?"

Then they touched.

Chapter 1

It took her thirty minutes to let her mind ease enough that she could think straight. Colleen didn't care for the man sitting across from her laughing it up like he'd heard the best joke ever. Trying to stand now that she was feeling a little better, she told him that he wasn't all that funny.

All they'd done was touch their fingers to each other. A normal greeting that everyone did. Put out your hand and expect a small bit of warmth, then you parted ways. But as soon as he touched her, she and he both had been knocked three ways from Sunday with her head pounding like a jackhammer.

Looking down on the man, Warren, she knew

who he was now, and he didn't look like he fared any better than she had. At least, she didn't think so. There was blood on his cheek, but the wound looked as if it had already healed. She asked him if he was all right.

Warren leaned back against the wall and casually crossed his legs in front of him. "No, this is starting to be a pattern. But something else that we can lay to rest, too, is that you're not my mate. What was that blast? This is the second time I've been knocked off my feet by a woman in this household, and each time I get a little more magic. I'm assuming that you did as well." Colleen told him that she did feel different. "I do as well. Like I've been energized and had the life sucked out of me at the same time."

"I do hope that you're not blaming that on me. I only meant to greet you." He said he had the same thing in mind when he'd put out his hand. "Well then, I don't have time to hang out here in the hallway with a rude man. I've things to — you told my brother about me being blackmailed, didn't you?"

"No. I didn't know about that at the time. I

only knew that you were broke. I'm happy that it turned out well for you." She told him that it was still ongoing, but the man wasn't bothering her any longer. "Then it's all good. I'm sorry if I—"

"You didn't do anything wrong. I'm glad that you did that for me. It's difficult for me to ask for help, so you made it easier on me. I did want to thank you for that." He told her that it was his pleasure. "I'm starting to feel some of whatever came to me in that blast. I can now feel where people are. Not their emotions, but just know that there is a man in town that is thinking about his late wife and what a terrible person she was to have saddled him with four children. I don't know the entire story, but just enough to make me want to go and help him. Or kill him. Until I figure out why he'd be thinking that, I'm withholding judgment for now."

"They're not his kids. Hers from previous relationships. I think we should take a walk over there soon and see what he might be doing to rid himself of his stepchildren." She put out a hand to help him up. He eyed it before he took it from her.

"I've no idea what we share now other than that, but I'm thinking that it's because of your brother."

"Hammy? What did he do? I'm going to kill him if he's set me up again. Well, he didn't do it the first time, but I thought he had." Shaking her head, she smiled at Warren. "Why do you think that what you and I got is from him?"

"Because I believe that he's a leader of a kiss. This one that is forming if I don't miss my bet. As his sister, you would have gotten magic as well as his mate. I think, no, I believe that's what is making Lander so strong. And since I'm a good friend of the family, every time I'm near or touch one of his family, he makes me more a part of the kiss. Does that make sense?" She nodded, then shook her head. "What part don't you understand? Or do you have a better explanation? If so, tell me. This is something that I've been thinking about for a while now."

"No. I mean, you're right, but I don't think he believes he's leader material. That didn't come out right. I think that he believes that because that's what we've been told all our lives, someone younger than the oldest living in a family cannot be a leader. So with grandda alive, he will believe that he's not able to become anything more than what he is right now." Warren asked her who told her that. "My entire family. All the way back, sheesh, Warren, all the way back as far as I can remember. My great uncle. Shane. He was very strong. Everyone thought that, well, not everyone but other families thought that he should have been running the family instead of my great grandda that had been. It certainly would have been more successful had he been. Safer, for sure. But since his father was still alive, he was never given a chance to...Christ, Warren. I think you might be right. And Hammy is stronger than Uncle Shane ever was. Especially since he has Lander at his side."

"As it should be. Did your uncle Shane have a mate?" She told him how he'd been killed one night while out with his father, and the opportunity had never come up for him. "He more than likely killed him because he was stronger." Warren looked at her, shocked. "I'm sorry. I don't know why I said that. I'm so very sorry."

"I think you might be right, however." She sat down on the chair that had seen better days and strengthened it up a bit with her magic when it wobbled. "So you think that Hammy is a leader. Yes, I can see that. I can also see him not understanding how it came to be. It would have been passed down to him, correct?"

"Yes. I mean, I'm not entirely sure how that would work, to be honest with you. I'm sure that there are books around or something that would tell us. But he's the strongest vamp I've ever encountered. And I've been around for a good long time." Colleen thought about the magic that she now had and told Warren about some of the things she'd only just discovered she could do. "We need to figure out if Shane was killed for his abilities. I haven't any idea why that would be important, but I think that it is. From there, I think we can narrow some things down to the point where we can make a couple of good cases to say that Hamish is our leader."

"No. I think first, we need to sit down with Hammy and talk to him about this. Grandda too. I have a feeling that he's under the same assumption as the rest of my family was." She liked that idea so much that she decided to call her brother to her. First, she warned Warren. "I'm not sure what sort of mood he's going to be in, but I think the sooner we can get this taken care of, the sooner we'll know what we're doing. It seems really important to me, almost like it's a matter of life or death that we see if Hammy is what we think he is."

She couldn't rid herself of that notion either. No matter how many times she tried to calm her mind from it, it wouldn't settle. As soon as Hammy told her that he was nearly to her, she felt a degree or two better. But it wasn't until she saw him and he was within touching distance that she felt he was safe. It was a feeling that she didn't care for, her being so worried about her older brother.

After talking to him about what they thought, he said what she had. That grandda would be the leader of the kiss if there was a need for one. That had been brought up too. Was there a need for one? She didn't know, but then she didn't hang out with many vampires but with families where it might be necessary. It was her feelings that made her think that yes, big brother, we do need to know if you're a kiss leader or not. Thinking about it, she had heard recently of some trouble in the next county.

"I wouldn't even know where to turn to ask anyone. I mean, there once was a library, but I don't think it's been around for a long time." Grandda said that Hammy should contact the council. "I thought about that too. Not for me, but some disciplinary things that I think need to be taken care of around the area. There are a few baby vamps that are going to be making trouble for all of us if they don't change their ways. You just call out to them for help, right?"

"Last I heard of it, that's how it was done. They might just want you to take care of it. If that's something that is needed." Warren shook his head almost as soon as he suggested that they'd want Hammy to take care of it. "I'd not do it, Hamish. Not without their personal backup or written out that you're in charge. That could come back to bite you in the ass too."

"Wait. I'm sorry. New to this stuff." They all smiled at Lander. She was such a wonderful person, but Colleen could tell she didn't understand why he had to ask to take care of the vampires. "What's a baby vamp? I'm assuming that I am. Whatever that is. Also, what sort of things are they doing out wherever that they need to be taken care of. And by taken care of, I'm assuming you mean they need to be killed. Correct?"

"They're draining humans." Colleen watched her new sister's face as what she'd said sunk in. "Yes. And then they leave the bodies there for anyone to come across. There are all sorts of rules that vampires have to follow so that they don't get into trouble. One of them is not to take blood from a human unless we compensate them in some way and ask permission. As you can imagine, asking for permission might be difficult at times. But we do help them out when they've given us enough of themselves to keep us alive. As for the baby vamps? I'm not entirely sure that they wouldn't get a second chance. That's what I don't know, either. How lax we've become as vampires that we need to take baby steps with the newer ones."

"I'm going to do this. Not just for my family, but you're right. Someone needs to be in charge. Not just of the babies but also of the elders too. There has to be accountability to them and for us, if they attack." Colleen stood up. Her entire being seemed to be frozen in place. When Hammy stood in front of her, she looked up at him. He was yelling at her to tell him what was wrong. "Colleen. You're starting to scare the shit out of—"

"They're coming. The vamps. They're coming here to confront you to take Lander. They know that she's strong." She could feel them as they surrounded the house. Not just them coming, but she could hear what they were talking about. How they were going to rape Lander and then put her out in the sun. "Call the council, Hammy. Before it's too late. Call them now."

They simply appeared in the room. There were three of them, and none of them looked a day older than fifteen or sixteen years old. Dressed in the garb of whatever era they were brought from, they looked around the room they were in as if they were just as surprised as she was that they were there. Hammy introduced the three newcomers to everyone in the room.

"Charles Hamish Perry, son of Charles and Maria Perry, now deceased. What is it we can do for you?" Colleen watched her brother as he explained about the vampires and what they were doing. When he pointed to her, Colleen said they were coming for Hamish by way of Lander, his mate. Only just remembering not to call him Hammy at the last minute, she told them what the conversation was they were having about Hamish's mate. "Do you wish for us to take care of them, young Hamish?"

"Who else would do it?" They conferred, the three of them did. "I don't know who is in charge of this area. Or, for that matter, the king of vampires. It's been a very long time. I will admit that I even cared about what was going on around me. I'm a loner most of the time."

"Why is it you think that you cannot take care

of them?" The middle person, a female child with considerable strength, asked Hamish also what he'd do with them. "You have been in charge since well before now, sir. Your father, he wasn't fit to be a leader, much less a king of vampires. It wasn't only him either but his mate as well. I do not mean to disparage your family, sir, but you yourself did not think of them much as parents, much less leaders."

"No. I didn't. And you're right. My mother was trouble." Hammy looked at Lander and then back at the speaker. "You said he wasn't a leader. I'll agree with that. But his father is still alive. Should he be in charge? I mean, I'm nothing more than a vampire with a family."

"You are so much more, Hamish Perry." The first child spoke with a huge smile on his face. "Since your birth, we have waited for you to come into your own. Since that day, we have been putting aside your dues and watching and waiting for you to come to us. Your parents were to bring you to us when you were in your early days."

"They never said anything." The third

child spoke then. Telling Hamish that they broke many agreements between them and the council. "Something that I'm going to be punished for? I hope not. I've only just gotten my life the way that I like it."

"Aulander was to come to you. We foresaw her being your mate. However, we never knew the time in which she would come to you. Again, we waited. She is, in her own right, a powerful mate. A good vampire and one that will command armies should it be necessary. With her at your side, Hamish Perry, you will rule the vampires forever. Ruling them in such a way that we'll have no more issues with the humans or their kind."

"I'm sorry. What did you just say? That I was supposed to be with Hamish? That you planned this all along?" The third child nodded. When Lander took a step towards the person, everyone else in the room took two back. For a slip of a woman, Lander already commanded armies. Her own. "You will have to explain to me just what you mean by that. Are you telling me that you had something to do with me being born and becoming his mate? And I would think hard on how you answer that if I were you. I'm not cattle to be sold off to the highest bidder."

"Oh no. That's not that at all. You were never thought of as anything but his queen." She asked the girl what that meant. "You are his queen. The mate to him as he is king. I don't think that you understand that Hamish is everything that we could have hoped for in a king."

"You believe him to be the king of vampires — all vampires of the world." It wasn't a question, but the girl looked around before nodding. "Then, with him being the king of vampires, which is what you believe, then that would make me the queen of vampires. As you said. Correct?" She nodded. "What use do I have of you three if there is a king and queen of all the vampires in the world?"

That shocked the three of them. Colleen had a feeling that they wanted Hammy to be king in the same manner as he was now. One that they could work around and — she hated to think about this — one they could blame for things that didn't go the way they should have. Nothing good was going to come from having the council right up her brother's ass. Colleen thought that the sooner they disbanded the merry lot of them, the better the world would be.

~*~

Robin put all the information in the computer and watched as it filled in the spaces that she hoped it would on the spreadsheet she'd been told to do. She'd been doing research in this hell hole since — well, longer than she could remember. Today she was having a good day as no one was around to bother her.

She'd not been born a clerk for the council. Robin had been born a vampire. To what she could remember, vampire parents. She'd had a brother and sister too, older than her by some years that she could barely remember either. But when she'd become twenty-five, the year she should have converted to her full self, nothing happened. She didn't have fangs. There was very little in the way of magic that belonged to her, and none of the things that should have frightened her, sun, wooden stake to the chest never bothered her. Robin was then considered a valueless female. One without worth.

No good family would allow her to associate with their sons. Not that it mattered to her. She wasn't one to socialize much anyway. Her parents and siblings had cut her off from them. Literally dropped her off at the council house, chained and tied like an animal so that they would destroy her. Destroy her as if she were nothing more than a cur. A bug under their—

"I have some research that I need for you to look up for me." She turned to look at the Idiot. Number one of the three council members that ruled her. "I wish for you to find me as much information on Hamish Perry as you can find. I'm looking for flaws."

"There are none." Idiot looked at her. "His family line is pure. One of the only vampire families that are. There are no flaws to his character nor to his family other than his papa and mother that are still out there. And there are rules about making the son responsible for their—"

The punch to her face sent her flying across the room. Tasting the coppery taste of blood in her mouth, she didn't bother wiping it away. Robin also knew that her face would remain bruised and battered until such time as it healed like a human would have that had been hit by a powerful being. There was no magic for her to heal herself. When she stayed on the floor, Idiot, the name that she'd given him centuries ago, stood over her.

"Did I ask you for rules? Did I say to you, slave, I needed to be reminded of the rules that govern him? No. I told you to find flaws." He drew back to kick her in the ribs, and she waited for the blow. When it didn't, she opened one eye to find herself in a very well-appointed office. With windows that looked out over an expansive yard. Also, there was a beautiful woman in the room.

"Hello." Scrambling away from the woman, she curled herself into a ball as close to the large desk as she could. After sniffing the air, Robin laid down on the floor, her throat exposed to the woman to allow her to rip it out or whatever she wished. She was, she realized, in the presence of the queen. "You must be Robin. To be honest with you, I had no idea—oh, do get up off the floor. I only wanted to have a nice conversation with you. I had no idea when I thought about having you here that you'd—who hit you?"

"You're the queen." The woman tisked at her while trying to get her up from the floor. "I can't be higher than you, my lady. It's forbidden."

"I've been looking over those idiocy rules that someone put...well, if you won't get up off the floor, I'll just join you there. Anyway. I was looking over the paperwork that I got this morning. I'm not entirely sure, I'm new to this magic, how they ended up on my desk, but there they are." Robin opened one eye and saw that the woman was indeed laying on the floor. Her head was only inches from her own. "That was when I saw your name. I'm so glad that you sign off on your work. It made it a good deal easier for me to call out to you. By the way, my name is Lander. Lander Perry. My husband, mate, I guess, is Hamish."

As she talked about the paperwork that had

appeared on her desk and the fun she was having finding things out, Robin felt herself relax more and more. While the other woman talked a great deal, it was all information that she'd been able to find and about how she had summoned her to come and help her.

"Idiot hit me. I don't know their names, but I have named them in my head. The first one is Idiot. The woman, who is terribly mean, is Moron. The third one, dumber by far than rocks in their garden, is Asshole." Robin watched as the woman sat up. Telling her to do the same. Robin had no choice but to comply. "They're angry with whatever happened here yesterday. They'll be all the more angry when they find out where I am."

"How long do you think it'll be before they figure out where you are?" Telling her that since she'd not told her where she was, which she shouldn't then, they'd not know either. "What do they pay you? I could use someone like you to do research for me. I'll double what they're paying you."

"I'm a valueless vampire, Lady Perry. I'm their

slave until I die." When her anger rose, palatable in the large room, Robin laid back on the floor. Her body was aching, trying to become one with the floorboards beneath her. "I'm sorry, my lady. Truly I am."

"I'm not upset with you, Robin. Here comes my husband and his sister. We'll get this taken care of right now. Mother fuckers. The three of them should be hung out to dry by their tits and balls." Robin couldn't help it. She laughed. "I'm glad to have made you laugh. It's that or cry sometimes, and this isn't a crying moment."

After she explained to the other two what was going on and how Lander had managed to bring her to her. Then she told them what she'd said about being valueless. It was like the room tightened when another man came into the large office with them. Backing away from the power that seemed to exude from him, Robin watched him as the stranger took his time coming toward her. Backing away as far as she could and still be in the room, she was terrified when he put out his hand toward her.

"I will never harm you, little one." She didn't move other than to drop her head down so that he'd not see the terror she was dealing with. "My name is Warren. I adopted the last name Justice because… well, I'm not really sure why I did that. But I belong to you. I'm your mate. You do understand that, don't you?"

"You don't want me." He said that he did. "No. As I was telling the others here, I'm worthless. I've been a prisoner to the council for reasons that you should understand. I'm a vampire, but in name only. I cannot bite or feed, nor does the sun bother me. I've never told anyone that. I think it's why I've been put in a windowless place for so—that doesn't matter. I'm not worthy of one such as yourself, Lord Warren."

"Who said this to you? Where have you been imprisoned?" She told him that she'd been turned over to the council when she'd not converted at the age of twenty-five. "That's the most…you do know that it more than likely means that your line isn't pure and that somewhere in your lineage, there was a human?"

"I have no way of knowing as they have never given me a last name or any name to work with to research it. It's been so long that I no longer—why do you even care about this? I cannot be your mate, Lord Warren. I've told you twice now that I'm not worthy of being with a vampire or anyone because of what I am." Just as she realized she was up in his face, poking him in the chest with her finger, he laid his hand over hers, and she felt the earth move under her feet. Whatever was happening, it was much more powerful than she could have done. She was going to get to the bottom of them right now. But he put his finger over her mouth.

"*Quiet.*" She heard the voices then. While unable to see Moron, she knew that the council was very close to where she was. "*They're looking for you. If they believe that Hamish or his mate is going to take their shit, they're going to be sadly mistaken soon. However, I don't believe they realize that you're here.*"

"*They wish for me to return.*" Warren nodded. "*I should return to my place with them. I belong to them until I die. They will punish me should they find me here. And you as well. I don't want that."*

"You no longer belong to anyone. You are free from anyone that thinks to have a hold over you. They'll get no satisfaction in trying to harm you, little one. They'll have to go through me to get to you, and that isn't going to happen. Nor will they be able to get by Hamish or Lander. As they have been told they are king and queen, I'm sure they'll use that so that you'll not return to them. Then, later, should you like, you can explain to me why you were considered unworthy when I think you the most precious gift in the world." She told him to stop teasing her. It was mean. *"I'm not teasing you, my love. I'm telling you straight up that I've, in this short amount of time, fallen in love with you. I will pledge myself to you and keep you safe for all eternity."*

Turning around so that she faced her bosses, she watched Idiot and Jackass acting like there wasn't anything amiss. She nearly giggled out loud when Lander asked them to have a seat. Like she was going to offer them tea or something. Robin could almost feel the anger coming off the vampire couple in the room.

While she knew she was hidden in the shadows of Warren's magic, it was fun to watch someone else have to deal with the three of them for a change. It occurred to her some minutes later that Hamish knew that one of them had been the one to hit her, but he didn't know which one as yet. He was trying to get that information out of them. She did wonder what they'd do to him once they figured it out.

"We've been wondering if you have the paperwork on your family. It seemed to have come up missing from the vaults." Hamish told Idiot that his wife was going over it. He started gathering things up when Lander smacked his hands away from them. "I'm not entirely sure why you'd think that you'd be better with the paperwork than we were, so I'll need to take that back with me. It is our property. My lady. We'll take it back and have it filed away. We have people for that sort of thing."

"How so?" Idiot looked at Lander and then back at Hamish when he asked again. "How is it your property when I'm the king? Shouldn't all this be mine? As you have said to me before, I'm the king, and my mate is the queen. I should be able to take what I want when I want it. Also, don't think that I didn't remember that you didn't answer me before when I asked you what use do I have of you if my mate and I are in charge. Why is it? Do you think that I should come to you when I need every little thing answered for myself?"

"No. 'Tis not that at all. But we've all the information you can ever want and can answer any questions you might have without you having to bother with the files. There is a system to the way things are given out and taken back. We'll just keep those for ourselves. That way, you won't have to bother with looking things up. You come to us, and everyone will be happy with the answers I give you." Lander told Moron that she actually did enjoy researching things. And that she was looking forward to it. Anger flashed quickly over his face for a second. Robin was sure that both Hamish and Lander had seen it too. "But you see, the files. You'll mess with the way things are for us, and that just will not do.

There is order in all this. An order that you will not be able to understand. Sometimes, even I can't understand the logic of the way things are filed. The person that we have helping us, well, they've made a shambles of everything. I don't suppose you've seen her, have you? The filing person that we use. She's quite stupid."

"You have a filing person? Oh, so that's why you don't know where things are. Because you don't, do you? It's because you didn't file them." It was a good question from Hamish, and she nearly giggled again. "Who is the name at the bottom of the pages? There is…what was that name, Lander? The name that keeps popping up at the bottom of each sheet? Did you write it—"

"There is no need for you to know anything about that stupid girl. That person, that thing works for us. It's said that she's addled." Lander asked why they'd have someone handicapped working on files. "Well, she does do that very well. But she isn't worthy of your praise. Why just yesterday, I had to reprimand her about getting too uppity. Her parents, well, you understand, sir, they didn't want anyone to know that they might well be associated with such a...thing. When I asked her to look into the purity of someone's lineage, she had the nerve, sir, to question me about it. Said that she knew the line by heart or something along those lines. No, she's not to be trusted with such things. I'll just take those things and file them away. I can't trust her to do it right. When I find her, and we will—"

"You've said that twice now. If you say I shouldn't trust her, yet you have her looking into files, then how should I trust you?" Idiot didn't seem to understand what Hamish was saying. The guy was an idiot, after all. "This girl that works for you. I'd like to meet with her. Perhaps you can set up a time for us to sit down in the filing rooms and go over what she has been doing with them."

"That won't be necessary." He reached once again for the paperwork that was on Lander's desk and, this time, was shoved away. "What are you doing to me? You've no right to treat me as such. I'm far smarter than you are. You can be king, sir,

I'll allow that, but you're not going to be harming me or the others. We'll have to think of a suitable punishment for—"

"Be gone." The room emptied of the three members. Had she not seen it with her own eyes, she might not have believed that there was anyone stronger than them. As it was, Lander looked directly at her and smiled. "I guess that clears one thing up. We are the king and queen of those idiots anyway."

Chapter 2

Warren didn't know what to think about the goings on in the house of Hamish. Today he found himself sitting out on the deck, just thinking about the last several hours. At some point, Robin had joined him out on the deck, and they were enjoying, at least he was the quiet of the afternoon.

"When I first came to the council house, they treated me less than a dog would be treated. I was only fed once a day, given water in a bowl, and I was only able to bathe when I could sneak out of doors in the evening rain. I could change my clothing when I wanted. But since I knew so little about the fashion of the day, I would end up wearing whatever soft clothing I could manage." Warren asked her how long she'd been in the filing room. "Centuries and centuries. It wasn't much of a room when I was first there. Just papers stacked up in corners or near the walls. But as more vampires were born or made, the room expanded for me to accommodate the files. It wasn't until recently, within the last few centuries, that I was able to figure out cabinets to use."

"I overheard you telling Colleen you found a catalog while out one night." She smiled at him. It was something that he wanted to see all the time. "I wondered how you were able to get things settled up so well down there. However, in the little time I was down there, I felt shut in. I don't know how you were able to endure that for so long."

She shrugged. "I didn't know anything different. I mean, I went from being in a large castle to being there, and that was it. I never, by my own accounting, fit in with my family. I believe that I was a disappointment to my mother from my first breath. She didn't care much for the fact that I was born with blond hair. And when it changed to this dark color, she thought me an oddity already. After not converting, I think that was the last straw for her to accept me." Warren asked about her father. "He was more of a yes ma'am than a father. Mother told him what to wear when to speak and what would come out of his mouth. I thought for sure, growing up, that he wasn't real. Just a puppet at the end of her strings. I don't think she liked me pointing that out to her either."

Warren shook his head. "No. I met them once. Long ago. They were at a party that I think my mother was throwing. They weren't invited. I do remember that much. Mom thought her terribly rude and an upstart. I hadn't any idea that there were three children with them at the time." She told him that she didn't go out much. "Yes, well, with them, I can understand that. Did you hear about the vampires from yesterday? I swear to you, Robin, I will laugh about that until I'm dust on the ground."

"I heard that they entered the house but nothing more. By then, I was trying to get the files back together that Idiot and Moron were messing with." Robin asked him to tell it to her. "Unless you'd rather not. I don't mind."

"They entered the house just as Lander dispatched the council. At the time, I hadn't any idea that the one that was supposed to be in charge was nothing more than a child. I'm to understand that Hamish is going to take care of whoever changed a ten-year-old into a vampire. There are rules, even if we don't know them all, that we must follow." Robin told him that all vampires, with their first breath, are given those rules to follow. "I guess I didn't know that part. But I can see where it would be helpful to someone—would you mind if I just held your hand? Just so I can feel closer to you?"

"Yes, of course." When she put her hand out to his, Warren kissed the back of it and then tucked it into his hand. "I never realized, but then why would I that a simple touch between mates could be so comforting. No, not comforting. Stabilizing. It's as if you've planted me or something. Pay no attention to me. I'm just being crazy."

"No, you're not. I feel the same way. Like you

said, you stabilized me. Put things that were in my head into order and made me feel better about, well, everything." He laughed a little, thinking about the story. "They came into the house as if they owned it. When Lander saw them standing there, these three children, she called for a nanny to take them away. Of course, as you can imagine, that didn't settle well with them. As soon as they took a step toward her, not even close enough to touch, she put out her hand and destroyed him."

"My goodness. The others must have looked shocked." Warren continued to tell the story while laughing. "Yes, I can see her doing that. Acting like she'd meant to do that all along. She's very intimidating, isn't she? I mean, I'm glad that she's on my side all the time. Then what happened?"

"There were six of them in total left. Once it was established that Lander wasn't going to take their shit, she sat down on the chair and let Hamish take over. I think it scared her a little, too, that it was so easy for her to destroy that child. She told us afterward that she could see the blood on his clothing and face from what he'd done to his maker." Robin let him pull her to his lap and hold onto her. "Hamish asked them what their plan was and how they thought it was going to fly now that he was in charge. None of them had an answer, but they did try and talk Hamish into letting them have Lander, as she was just the mother figure that they wanted. It didn't end well for the others when he told them that she was his mate and that they needed to respect them. The children, because that was all they were, didn't think that Hamish would harm them because of what they were. I guess no one will make that mistake again with him."

"He destroyed them all after that." Warren nodded. "I feel for him. It would have been difficult to destroy an illusion like that. I'm sure someone knew the plan the maker had."

"Hamish did. I think that Lander did as well, but when he told me later about how the maker made the children to get into the house so that he could, he was pissed. But when they killed their maker, things didn't bode well for any of them. I suppose that we're lucky that they didn't do more harm than they already did." Robin nodded but didn't move off his lap. "We should talk about a few things. If you'd like. I have a house, a few of them, but it's up to you if you want to live in any of them."

"I don't know what I'm doing right now. It's all so sudden. Just a few days ago, I was working as a slave to the council. With no hope of meeting anyone and becoming a mate to someone as powerful as you are. Now I'm not sure what my role is in things like that. I do know that the council is back at the place I was staying, but I'm not sure what they're doing." Warren told her that Hamish had taken all the files and cabinets out of the building. "Yes, he told me this morning. They're in a cave deep in the mountain for safekeeping. He has set up the computer that I made in one of his offices downtown. He wants me to keep working on the files but to get paid for doing it."

"I hadn't realized that you weren't being paid either. He's looking into having all your back wages given to you." Robin, just as he knew she would, said that wasn't necessary. "It is to him. No one should work for free when they're doing something like you were doing. Also, I wanted to tell you before I forget again my parents are coming here in a couple of days. I thought they'd be here by now, but I guess they got hung up at some meeting. I don't know. My parents are an oddity, but they're good people."

"I do want to talk to Hamish about something. I've been trying to think of a way to have it brought up. He seems to be under the impression that his parents are both deceased. They're not. His father is. He died some time ago. But his mother is alive and well." Warren said that he was sure that Hamish didn't know that. "I didn't think so. I need to get on that soon. She's planning to come here soon as well. I don't know if she'd feel if he was suddenly the king of all vampires, but something has alerted her to a change."

"Could it be that he's found his mate?" Robin asked if that was something that would cause magic to notify her. "Yes. I mean, when I spoke to my parents, they already knew that you'd found me. They said they felt the same thing that we did.

That I was settled." Warren laughed. "I'm going to have to think of another way to put that. It makes me sound like I'm settled down with fifty children or something."

They sat out there and talked about different things for several hours. Warren hadn't been able to find the time to just talk about things in a long time. It wasn't as if he was just too busy but finding someone to just talk to that didn't try to outshine or outdo him was something that he missed. Hamish was another person that he could talk to like that. As well as Lander.

She was becoming someone that he could trust too. There were few people that he could rely on. His parents, for sure and Hamish, of course. There wasn't anyone that he felt like he could just tell something to and not have it spread all over the world before he was finished speaking. Sometimes, like today, he just wanted to talk and perhaps to vent. However, he did notice that the two of them weren't venting so much as making future plans.

"I've never lived in a house before. I mean, I

did with my parents, but it was more of a place to sleep than anything else. They didn't offer me any comforts of a home. I suppose I could have asked for them or made some of it on my own, but it never bothered me overly much that I wasn't a part of the family. I haven't any idea why but that's all I remember about them. Hamish seems to think that the family line isn't as pure as I believe I was told. But since I have no names to go with it, I can't find anything about them." She looked at him. "I'm sure that it'll matter to your parents whatever there is in my lineage. I know that your line is almost as pure as Hamish's is. There is only one other family that hasn't a single outsider in their family line, and it's the Phelps family. But I think that they have pretty much died out."

"Murray Phelps?" Robin nodded. "I know of the man but not a great deal about him. I think that he's friends with Hamish. We've been friends forever, but there are a few of his buddies that I didn't get to know all that well. There is a man by the name of Kirk too. His name is Brad Kirk. It's my understanding that he was instrumental in saving a few vampires once, and they gave him immortality. I don't remember all the details on it, but he wasn't all that thrilled with the gift. He would be a human that is coming here to work for Hamish. Do you know of him?"

"I don't. I'm sorry. But I can have a look if you'd don't mind." Robin pulled out a small tablet and put in the name Kirk. "Here it is. He's been honored by the bear council for bravery beyond measure. The vampires did give him immortality for his help at some kind of raid once, but he lives with the human sector for most of his life. According to this, he's been around since the early seventeen hundreds, and you're right. Isn't thrilled about being around for so long."

"What does that say he's been doing?" She slid her fingers over the keyboard for a couple of minutes before she told him. "A bit of everything then. I would imagine that Hamish knows that and will use him for a lot of different things. I hope that he can come to help him. Or help them both out."

"Yes, I can see where Hamish would like to have his friends around him and happy. I don't know how happy some of them will be, but he's going to be glad that they're here." Robin looked behind them when the door opened and then closed. "Hello, Hamish. We were just talking about you. I have a bit of news for you if you'd like it."

"Good or bad?" She told him that she thought he'd think it bad news. "It's been a hell of a morning for that so far. The council idiots are hounding me to find you, too, by the way. Be careful of them." She told him that she would. "Good. What's the news?"

"Your mother is on her way here. She's been in Europe for the last fifty years or so. Hiding out from the council. I'm not entirely sure why but that's what I was able to find out when I was told to look for flaws in your lineage." He asked her if she had killed his father. "No. Not that I can see in the paperwork. There is blame put on her by Idiot, but there isn't anything connecting her to his death. Not anything that I can see anyway. But she is coming here."

~*~

Maria watched the house for another few minutes before venturing out into the weakening light. She knew that her son lived in the big house. It was all over the papers that he'd purchased the home some weeks ago. Also that he had a wife. While she wasn't sure of the latter of the two things she'd found out, something had pulled her here to come and see him.

Risking everything wasn't something that she did often. Rarely, as a matter of fact. But the pull to go and seek his help was making her do things that she normally would never do, like coming out of hiding.

When Charles was killed, she'd been hurt as well. Actually, she thought that she was as dead as he was. Maria still had no idea who had put her to ground to heal. Nor did she know why they'd done it. However, she was as grateful as she'd ever been. It had changed her lifestyle. Not to mention everything about her personality as well. Making her way to the house across the street, she was startled when a woman appeared in front of her.

"You've been lurking about for days. Wouldn't

it have been easier just to pick up a phone and call? Or to have reached out to him?" Maria fell to the ground and exposed her throat to the woman in front of her. "Why is it that everyone drops to the ground like I'm going to stamp all over you. Get up. Christ, it's like talking to a jack in the box all the time around here lately."

"You're the queen of vampires. I can do no less than to show you respect." The woman told her that if she wanted to show respect, then there were better ways of doing it rather than getting all muddy. "It's the way we were trained."

"Well, get over that shit." Maria had no idea why but she liked this woman. "I'm Lander Perry. Mate to your son. I wanted to come out here and establish that I'm going to kill you if you fuck with either him or Colleen. I love them both dearly, and I won't have them harmed because of you."

"I won't harm either of them. Colleen is here as well?" Lander just stared at her. "You're not very nice, are you? I don't mean to be rude, I'm actually kind of enjoying your outspokenness, but you are rude."

"It cuts a lot of bullshit out of conversations when I have to get to the bottom of things. Your father-in-law is here too. He's not as blunt as I am, but I will tell you that he has no reason to believe that you had nothing to do with the death of his son. I don't know why but I have a feeling that you didn't." She told her that she'd not had anything to do with his death. "We'll see. For now, I'm going to give you the benefit of the doubt and not simply destroy you right where you stand. But what I said about harming them holds true. I will destroy you in ways that will be written about for decades, if not forever."

"I promise you that I'll be on my best behavior." She told her that she'd better be. "If you'd allow it, I'd like to see my children. I've been down for so long that I've missed a great deal of their lives. I'm assuming, like most of the vampire world, they thought me dead as well."

"You still might be to them. The verdict is still out." As she offered her to go ahead of her, the younger woman continued speaking. "There is a room set up for you. I'm assuming that you can take a bit more sun than other vamps. If you don't like the room, there are others that you can pick from."

"I'll take whatever you can give me." Nodding, Lander followed her into the house. "You might know this already, but I don't know what happened to Charles. Nor who put me to ground to heal."

"I do. However, I'm not going to tell you just yet. I have other things to work out. I can see things, Maria. Not just what happened that day but also who took care that you didn't die as well." Thanking her, Maria turned when someone cleared their throat. "This is Warren Justice and his mate Robin. They're guests here, too, until their home is finished. They've only just met. Tomorrow a man by the name of Calhoun Meyer is coming to be interviewed for the position of a psychiatrist at the clinic that my father funded. I know nothing more about him than that."

"Thank you." When she felt her son enter the room, it was all she could do not to drop to the floor as she had with his mate. It was the threat of smacking her stupid if she did that that kept her on her feet. The bear hug that she received from Hamish was much more than she expected and so needed that she sobbed while he held her.

Colleen joined them in the hug. Whatever she had expected of her children, this wasn't it. To have been welcomed at all was a surprise. To have them there to hold her while she blubbered about how much she had missed them was something that she would cherish for the rest of her days.

Pulling apart finally, she held their hands as they stood in the front hallway. Maria noticed they'd been left alone, and when she was led to a nice living room, she sat down on the big couch with them on either side of her. She told them everything that she could remember about the day that their father had been killed and what she'd been doing since then to survive.

"Lander has this ability to see things that I can't. Not really in the future, but she can locate and figure out clues from what she can see. She told me that someone had buried you in the deepest cave in the richest soil that was there. Also, had on two different occasions moved your body so that no one would find you." She asked Hamish if he knew who it was or why they'd done that. "Not yet. She's still looking into things. I know that I can look to see what she's found, but I'd rather keep my teeth where they belong. Lander has threatened me on more than one occasion of pulling out my fangs and beating me to death with them. I love her very much, but she scares the shit out of me too."

When they were joined by the rest of the household, she saw that Charles, her father-in-law, was holding himself back from her. She didn't blame him. Maria knew what sort of person she'd been before all this had happened. Making small talk with him seemed to help. Right up until he stood up. She did as well.

"Did you have anything to do with his death? Lander says nay, but I know you better than anyone in this room. If you did, then don't you lie to me and tell me something that'll make you seem like you've had a switch up in your life." She told him that she'd had nothing to do with his death. "I don't want to believe you. As I said, I know you better than most. But I'm going to let you go for now. But if I find out you've been lying to me, Maria, I'll hunt you down and take care of you."

"We were talking, the two of us. Walking along the path that led to the back of our home. That morning we had witnessed the killing of six vampires. A family that had been selling their blood to humans for money. The council had pulled them from their home and had laid them out in the sun. No straps, no chains, just tossed them out of their home into the blazing sun. Charlie and I spoke about how that could very well have been us for all the things that we'd been guilty of in our lifetime." Charles asked her if she had sold her blood. "No. I'd like to say that we'd never do anything like that, but I have no idea what we might have done had we been…we decided to change our lives around. Get ourselves in a better position so that we could make our children proud of us. The adult children of that family, they were killed as well when the council decided that the family line would end that day. It was the most severe punishment I'd ever witnessed."

"They weren't selling their blood to humans." Everyone turned to Robin when she spoke up. "I was never able to research much more than the events up until that day until recently. Once the family had been killed, their physical records disappeared with them. All lineage was destroyed in that second. But they weren't selling their blood to anyone. As far as I could tell, they'd been in no trouble up until that morning."

"Then why were they killed? Do you know?" Robin turned to Lander, and at her nod, Robin said that she did. "Please? Will you be able to tell us?"

"They were the Winehouse family. Not too terribly old vampires, but they were struggling to make things work for them. The council, the one that is currently in office, decided that they wanted to make sure to set an example of them by killing off a couple of them. The blood selling was a lie so that they could justify their deaths. However, once they started tossing the adults out into the sun, it was more fun than they thought it would be and killed the rest of them as well. After that, the council started targeting other families, those that would cooperate with them in selling off vampire blood to the highest bidder. It was a way for them to make a great deal of money in a very short amount of time."

"But vampire blood doesn't work that way. Once it leaves the body of a vampire, it's no longer useful. It might well have been water." Robin told Hamish that she knew that too. "I'm sorry. I have a feeling that you know a good deal more about our kind than anyone else."

"No. Not really, but the council did figure out, almost too late for them, that they couldn't sell off vampire blood. That at some point, it would just disappear. Or worse yet, it would mix with the body of a human and make them wish for death. So they began making their own version of the blood. Mixing water with anything they could get their hands on that tinted the water a dark blood color." It was Hamish that seemed to understand what was going on first. "Yes, you got it. They were killing humans in a way that wouldn't come back to it being a vampire.

In doing so, as the council, they were free to go about their business, and no one was the wiser."

"Did you know this before today?" Robin said that she'd not known anything until she found Maria that day. "You buried my mother then. You put her in a place to keep her safe."

"I did. The council decided after killing her mate that if she found out that they had saved her from death, then your mother would be beholden to them. She'd do just about anything to make some money. They had no idea that she'd had a change of heart and wouldn't help them. But they were banking on what she'd been like before. I took her body from where they had put her, put some ash in the container she was in and put her in the caves. They thought that she'd been killed when someone opened the doors. It wasn't always easy to keep her safe, but I managed to make sure that she was at least safe from them."

"I can't thank you enough for that." Maria did have a great deal to be thankful for but right now, she wanted to know what was going to happen to the council for what they did to the Winehouse family. "I'd like to help all I can. Anything you need of me, I'll do it. I want them to be punished."

"They will be. For now, we're gathering information. I am, at least. Once I have enough, I'm going to present it before the king and the council, and he will decide what to do with them." Everyone turned to Hamish. "He's going to be objective in this. After being presented with all the information, he'll decide what needs to be taken care of with them, and they'll be dealt with accordingly."

"I want them gone anyway, so this is the right way to do this." Robin pointed out that he wasn't being objective. "No, I'm not, but I've seen enough with this to know that they're not going to be around much longer. I'd like to be able to make this so that they don't just end up in a vampire prison and are being dealt with completely. As in, their deaths need to be public so that everyone knows that I'm the new king."

"I'm so very proud of you, son. So would your father have been." His embarrassment was great, and

Maria wanted to laugh. But she held onto her humor, afraid that she might piss him off when things were going so smoothly right now.

Maria was shown to her room and fell in love with it. There wasn't anything that she'd change in the pretty blue room. As she lay down on the bed, just to test its comfort, she thought of all the things that she'd been told tonight. The council was in for a big surprise, she knew. And once they were exposed, she knew that they would be. She'd feel easier about living around here. Not that she was sure it was them following her, but they seemed to be the most likely people. Maria was going to lay low here too. There wasn't any sense in making waves when things were being taken care of by someone else.

Chapter 3

Warren waited for his parents to show up last night and into today. He'd contacted them just a few minutes ago and was asked to wait for a few minutes before they could speak. He wanted his parents to be there now, but he did understand that it wasn't just a simple thing of them just showing up when he wanted them to. There were other things that kept getting in their way. Like their mode of travel to the house.

Just last night, he'd been told that his home was ready for him and Robin to move into. The walls had been sanded down, and the rich smell of warm wood permeated the entire house. His parents rooms were ready, too, and that made him happy. Robin was a bit nervous, but she told him that if they gave her any shit, she'd wipe up the floor with them. He really loved that woman.

"*Son, what do you know about the council wanting us to pay dues for coming to see you? We were told not to ask questions of this new rule as it would upset the reigning king. But I've known Hamish since he was nothing more than a child, and I know that he doesn't need the money no matter what they say about him.*" He asked his dad how much the dues were. "*Ten thousand dollars. In small bills, if you can believe that.*"

"*There are all kinds of fishy things going on with the council. Hamish is looking into things here. When do you have to pay them? Did they tell you?*" His dad told him that he wasn't able to cross into the state without the money. "*I wonder if this idiot knows that we can cross into the state without his knowledge? What do you want me to do?*"

"*I'll be where you are in a second. I'm bringing my mate with me too.*" He wasn't sure what was going to happen once Robin was outed as being with him, so he made sure that Hamish was aware of what was going on as well. *"They're not being subtle about it either. Just telling them that they need ten grand as you're broke and need the money."*

"I'll meet your parents there with you. Bring Robin if that wasn't your plan." He said that it was. "Good. I've had about enough of their bullshit. It's time for them to just be gone."

Showing up with Robin where his parents were, he was glad that Robin made a big show of being with him. He could tell that the council was pissed off. Especially Moron. When they asked her why she'd not been doing her job, she simply ignored him in order to welcome his parents to their home. They were walking back to his car when Moron stepped in front of his dad.

"Weren't you warned about talking about this with anyone?" Dad asked him what he was talking about. "I told you that the king is embarrassed about his status as a poor man, and you weren't to blab it to anyone else but just the two of us."

"Three if you count my wife. And I didn't blab

anything. I simply asked my son a question. You don't expect me not to get all the information that I can before giving you any money, do you? I mean, what sort of fool do you take me for?" Moron looked at him, and Warren smiled at him. "This is my son and his mate. I've come here to see them if the king isn't available. That is what you said to us, wasn't it? That without the dues to him, Hamish couldn't see us. So, since we were here, my wife and I decided to see our son instead."

"But he's a friend of the king." Dad just stared at Moron. "I didn't want him to know that we're collecting money?"

"So he has no idea that you're trying to scam people out of their hard-earned money?" Hamish showed up then. By his side was his mother, sister as well as Lander. Of all of them, Lander looked the most amused. "Hello, Hamish. I didn't know that you were going to meet us here. I wonder how much this man will charge us if you've come to see us?"

Warren didn't move when Moron and Idiot both told Robin to get back to her job. If they touched her, he was going to kill them all. But all he did was get into her face and yell at her about people's heads going to roll once he was in charge of things. Hamish asked him what he was talking about.

"You're the king, and you're not playing fairly. Why are you questioning our every move? Why don't you just do what you're supposed to do and let us run things? It would have worked had…your uncle did the same thing. Always butting his nose into things that were of no concern to him. Do you have any idea how long it took us to get him killed? Just go back to your home and let us handle this transaction. If you don't, then you might find yourself dead and ash too." Idiot and Jackass both seemed to understand that Moron had gone too far in her rant. They were pulling on her sleeve and telling her to hush up. "Damn it, leave me alone so that we can make some money, real money for a change." She turned back to Hamish. "Well? What are you still doing here? This is no way for us to be partners in things. Go back to being the lazy king that we want you to be." Hamish shook his head before speaking to them.

"I tried very hard to give you three the benefit of the doubt. Trying my best to see some sort of good in you. A redeeming quality that would make it seem justified not to destroy you. But you've admitted to so many crimes so that you could be in power over those that you were to serve. What saddens me the most is that you've no care at all what you've done to the lineage of so many people. Council three, I order your death by fire."

It was such a simple thing to say, but it had the power to end all three of their lives. Even as Moron was set on fire, she was screaming at Hamish to take it back, to go away. When they were gone, nothing but bits of clothing and jewels that had been adorning their clothing, no one moved for several minutes.

The room seemed to expand and then shrink several times in a matter of seconds. Watching Hamish, he saw the exact moment when he was king in reality. He had been before, but now it was a fact.

As his body was lifted from the floor, he bent back almost in half. It was then that he noticed that Lander was in the same position. Her long hair floated down to almost reach the floor as it changed color. A wide white streak appeared where there had been none before.

He felt magic roll over him. Akin to his first time becoming a vampire. After all this time, he knew that it was the same feelings and emotions that came with it. Not that he was becoming a vampire again, but he was becoming more of one. Stronger and more knowledgeable about protecting Hamish and his mate. Closing his eyes against the pain that the information caused in his head, Warren blindly reached for something to hold onto and was happy when his hand connected with Robin.

When he woke, he was lying next to Robin in a bed he'd not been in before. Sitting up caused him a great deal of pain, but he was able to look around. Sitting on the side of the bed, he was glad for the lessening of pain, but he still had no idea where he was. Pulling her around to sit on his lap, Warren felt better when Robin wrapped her arm around his waist and laid her head on his chest.

Robin groaned as she stretched her sore

muscles. "I do believe that I'm broken." He laughed, feeling better all the time. "I don't suppose you know where we are, do you? I've only been in one of the rooms of Hamish's home, but this wasn't it."

Warren looked around the room, then shrugged when nothing looked familiar to him either. "I haven't a clue. Let me see if I can find anyone around close that might have some answers." He kissed her then, feeling the need to do so like he needed his next breath. "Or I can just sit here with you and work up the energy to make love to you. Not that it would be too much of an effort, mind you, but I'm not going to rush you into anything."

Robin smiled at him. "I know what you mean. However, I have to tell you something. I've fallen in love with you. I guess it was a wonderful thing that those fools held out for me to come to you, but I hate the way that they did it." He told her how much he loved her as well. "You reach out. While you're doing that, I'm going to go to the bathroom. Maybe that will ring a clue into my overstuffed head."

Warren waited until she left him before he

reached out. Really, all he wanted to do was pull Robin back into bed and spend the rest of his life there. But life didn't revolve around having sex all the time, more the pity. He reached for Hamish.

"How are you feeling?" He told him that he wasn't sure just yet. *"Yeah, right there with you on that. I've been feeling like I've been run over and zapped at the same time. Lander is taking another nap. She's been sleeping off and on all day. Where are you, by the way?"*

"I was hoping that you could tell me. I've not got a clue. Just woke up in this bedroom with Robin next to me. Neither of us know where we are. Or, for that matter, how we got here." Hamish asked him what was the last thing he remembered. *"Seeing you and Lander being lifted up. Oh, and her hair turned white in a long streak. Did that happen?"*

"Yes. I have one, too, but it's not as noticeable as hers is. When she woke up about an hour ago, she was liking it. Also, she's stronger with magic. I'm assuming that the streak is to mark her as my mate, but I haven't any idea." Robin came out of the bathroom and said that she could hear the two of them talking. *"I can hear her*

too. Okay. Do you know what's going on?"

"I do, as a matter of fact. I also know where we are. We're at the home that Warren had picked out. I'm not sure how the finishing touches were done while we were done, but it's so that we don't have to worry about the house when there are — you should know that Warren and I are your protectors. I believe that we would be called your seconds. I'm to watch over Lander, not that I think she needs it, but Warren will be there for you. The white streak is to show that you're now and forever able to sustain any kind of hit to your body. I'm thinking so that someone can see it and make a choice about wanting to come at you or not. I don't know. Begs to wonder why you're going to need us, but that's what I know. Also, because of us being what we are to you, we're immortal as well. Like, you can still have your head removed, but nothing else will kill you off. I'm sure you can take on more sun already with your age, but this will help you to blend in more." He asked her why they'd have to blend in more. *"Because as king ding-dong of all past and future vampires, there will be a great many more people out there that will want you dead. I'm assuming, only knowing you for the little bit*

that I do, that this is something that occurs a great deal with you."

"*Very funny.*" She laughed and sat down with Warren on the bed. *"About an hour ago, some boxes showed up here. I've not gone through them yet, but they're all marked in order of opening them. Have any idea what that might mean?"*

She didn't know but asked if they could be there when they were opened. Hamish said that he'd like that as well. As they were getting ready to leave the house, talking to Hamish at times or just each other, he liked how they were slowly getting to know one another. They seemed to be very comfortable too with each other. It occurred to him that they were becoming friends before they were lovers. That could only mean good things for the two of them, he thought.

"Your parents are at the house too. I didn't mention that earlier, but they seem to be settling in well." Warren told her how Maria was doing the same at Hamish's home. "He didn't seem all that surprised or even shocked to know that she was alive. I wonder why not."

"Maria hasn't been on good terms with anyone for a long time. When she said that she's changed, that too is something that she's tried to win people over with, and it fails every time. The fact that she is still alive probably didn't bother Hamish because she was forever pulling stunts like that one. I remember once when she and Charles both pretended that they'd been kidnapped, and Hamish had to pay a great deal of money to get them free. They were no more kidnapped than I was at the time, but they used the money that he'd paid to take a long and lavish vacation. I don't know that he's ever forgiven them for that." Robin said that she didn't know that she could forgive them either. "I'm not saying that she's not changed, but I'd not get too involved in her life. I think that's what Hamish is doing. I'm not worried about her taking advantage of him again. Lander will end her before anything harms Hamish."

"Good. Lander is sort of scary, isn't she? Last night she was telling me what she does for the police and other agencies. Her being able to connect with people has helped her in her retrieval of people a great deal, she told me." Warren said that he thought that she was the best there was. "Not to hear her talk about it. She seems to think that the world can go on without her, and she's not be missed."

"I got that about her too. But I do love her like a sister. I might be able to hold my own in a conversation about vampires, but she can broach any subject and be well-versed in it. Like I said, she's scary." They were both laughing when they got to Hamish's house. As soon as they entered the living room, she whistled. "There are a lot of boxes. And I've seen these before. These are boxes of the dead, their accounting of the money that they have put aside for their loved ones to use once they're gone."

"I thought as much. The records are well written. I just peeked in one of the boxes. I'm assuming you had something to do with how well things are written down?" Hamish handed her one of the smaller boxes when she told him she'd been doing that forever. "I found this one right away. I believe this is your family. I didn't know that when

I pulled it off the top of the stack. But as soon as I touched it, I knew you needed it. Take your time reading it over. Also, I'd like to talk to you about how you figured out computers and files to put this stuff in. That way, I can get it taken care of before it takes over my home."

"I can do that too." Handing him the box, Robin asked him to send it to their home. He knew she wasn't keen on embarrassing herself in front of anyone, so he did just what she wanted. Warren could feel her emotional turmoil as she handed off the box to him.

~*~

"I guess all I wanted to do was to figure out a way for the computers to work for me and made it happen. To be honest, after reading the specs and what a computer could do for me, I didn't have a clue. But it said that it could hold copious amounts of data, and I went with it." Lander asked her how she'd come up with the spreadsheet. "Oh, that was easy. Once I started playing around with what it would do, these places popped up on it that showed me all kinds of shit I could make the computer do. Not with programs. I don't have the slightest clue on how to write one of those. But I figured that if I were to tell it what I wanted it to do, magically, then it would be all right. When I first started working with it, I figured that I'd be the only one that worked with the computer, so it mattered little how I got it to work."

"You taught yourself how to input data and made it come out the way you wanted it to, correct?" Robin nodded at Lander. "While I think that's brilliant, I also think that it's wonderfully amazing that you were able to make it work. Not that you couldn't, but that you knew what you wanted it to do and how to get it working. I don't know that I would have been able to do that. Hell, it's doubtful that anyone would have been able to make that work as well as you did. You're talented."

Turning her back on her friend, she mumbled about how it had been easy with the books in front of her. Not that they were all that helpful. It wasn't as if she'd gone to college or even to have finished high school. She'd been born a female, and that had started her out on limitations on what she was allowed to do or not do.

Being able to sneak out at night was what had saved her from all kinds of trouble. That was when she found the thing called the internet. It had taken her all kinds of questions, pushing humans to answer them for her until she slightly understood what it was. Then it took her another six months of trial and error to get it to work for her. Finally, like the computer, she just made it do it.

The internet nearly got her killed a while back. Robin just couldn't fathom having this little wire attached to the computer that would open up information that was just out there for everyone to see. For an entire year, all she did was search for things.

Work piled up so badly that she had to work three years straight, day and night, just to get things in order. Even after all that time, she would still find files that she'd shoved out of her way in favor of looking for things. Robin had gotten to, right from her little hovel, see how things were put together and left standing by just asking the computer to find it for her.

"Have you gotten a chance to go over your parent's information yet?" Telling Lander that she wasn't sure she wanted to know after all this time. "I can understand that. They didn't do right by you, and I'd have a hard time even wanting to know anything about them. My mother is in prison, did I tell you that? I'm going there soon so that I can tell her that my dad left me all kinds of money, and I'm using it to put together a place for people to get a second chance at life. Like you, learning the computer."

She was helping them out at the teaching center. It was also a place for men and women to dry out. There were a lot of people there that she enjoyed talking to. Some of them, almost all of them, were lonely. They no more cared about learning a new thing than she had when she'd been around their age. The people of the generation that was seeking companionship had seen so much in their short life that she was sure that they'd had their minds blown quite enough.

She and Lander were sorting through the
boxes that had been delivered to Hamish's home.
Mostly it was to set them in order by the numbers on
the top of them. After they got ten of them stacked
up, Lander contacted the family to ask them what,
if anything, they wanted to be done with the money
that had been set aside for them. A lot of the families,
like the one that she was looking at now, had no one
left. She asked Lander what was going to happen to
that money.

"It'll be set aside to use for family emergencies.
I never realized that there still is a great deal of
trouble out there for vampires. That money will
get them identities as well as a place to live where
no one has any idea what they are. Sad really that
still in this day and age, we still have to hide from
what we are." Robin told her that she'd seen a great
deal of it in her time on this planet. "I bet you have.
I can't even imagine the things that you've seen or
witnessed. Even being locked up the way that you
were, I'm sure that you weren't able to see as much

as you wanted to see."

At dinner time, she made her way home. They were beginning to see the end to the boxes now, so they didn't mind cutting out early to head home. All the boxes had been stored in one of the larger buildings near their home so that they could keep an eye on them. Not that she thought that anyone could understand what they were looking at, all the information was in the vampire language. Still, it was good that they were making sure that families got what they needed.

The closer she got to their home, the more exhausted she felt. Robin supposed it was because she was sleeping so little, worrying about the information that Hamish had given her about her parents. As soon as she got home and figured out that Warren wasn't home, she pulled the box from the shelf and opened it. Whatever was in it didn't mean all that much to her anymore, but she might as well get it finished up.

The first thing she saw was documentation of her birth. Not a birth certificate as humans had but signed paperwork saying that she'd been born to such and such parents. There was a year—much to her surprise, she was older than she thought, as well as who was there as a witness. A brother and a sister-in-law plus a sister. Her parents' names were Alford and Ginger Hanson. Her brother was Bentley, his wife was Alma, and her sister was Constance.

"What are you looking at?" Showing Warren what she had, he told her they were all alive except the sister. "If they were dead, it would show up as red ink rather than black. You might not care what happened to her, but if you can find a picture of her or something, I can find out for you. I got this ability from Lander."

"I'm not sure what I want right now. I wasn't sure that I even wanted to look at it but figured I'd get it over with." He sat down next to her and pulled out the paperwork on her birth. Under it was more paperwork. "Look at this. This is the paperwork that turned me over to the council idiots. It says here that I was to be killed by them, not used as a slave."

The more they dug into the box, the more she

hated her parents. There were notes from them to the council that said how she was a horrific child. When she'd been nothing but an infant. That she was casting spells. She wasn't a witch but a vampire. How did they explain that away? Lots of things in the box that painted her into a terrible situation from the day she was born.

While she was putting things in order, she realized that her line wasn't nearly as pure as the paperwork claimed. Not only were there humans sprinkled throughout her lineage, but there were also other shifters. The one that made her laugh the most was the bear shifter who married and sired her father.

"I only remember this now because he was terrified of bears his whole life. I wonder if his father chased him around or something to aggravate him. They did that to me, my family. Because I couldn't do much other than hiss at them when they knocked me around." They both got a laugh out of it. "I wonder why I wasn't killed. I mean, there are all sorts of times when I was threatened with death, but no one ever followed through. Back then, I would have been happy about it. Not now, but when I was a slave to them. Then a slave to someone else."

"They found a use for you and kept you around, I guess. I'm very glad that they did. I wouldn't have survived without you in my life. That goes for now too." Warren leaned back in the chair that he'd been sitting in. "My parents want us to get together tonight if you're all right with that. They just want to rest up from yesterday a little more. I think that it upset my dad more than anyone. Not that he was targeted but that the king of vampires had to intervene. I don't think that he wanted to bother him about it. Something so trivial, he said."

"I think when my in-laws are threatened, everyone should intervene. Including the king and queen if necessary." She got up and sat on his lap. She found so much comfort sitting with him or on his lap that she wondered how she could make that happen all the time. Robin buried her face into his neck and felt his pulse start to pound. "I want to talk to you about a couple of things, like sex. I've never had it before. Not that I ever had the opportunity to have it, but I've not. However, I want you to know that having it with you is about all I can think about. Sex, I mean."

He pulled her head up from his neck and then wiped away the tears. She wasn't just embarrassed that she told him what she had but that he wasn't going to enjoy sex with a centuries-old virgin. She told him that.

"Oh, honey." He kissed her gently on her mouth and then held her in his arms. "I love you, Robin. So very much. And for as much as I want to make love to you, not just have sex, I know that it's going to be epic. But only when you're ready."

Squirming on his lap, he told her to behave. Putting her forehead to his, he lifted her face up again and kissed her. It was, she thought, the sweetest, most deliciously amazing kiss she'd ever had. The man could make a saint want him, she thought.

"How about we go over and see my parents for a couple of hours. You and I will walk home then—and only if you want to—I will chase you up the stairs to our bedroom, and we will have some bonding time. Not that I'm not enjoying canoodling with you all the time, but my poor cock thinks that he's being left out of some fun with me jacking off every few hours just to be around you." She looked at him, and he closed her mouth. "I'm joking, love. It's only about five times a day."

They were both still laughing when they set out for his parent's hotel. They had been going to stay at their home but decided that they wanted to be able to come and go when they pleased. That was fine with Robin. She had no idea if she was going to be noisy or not and didn't want to have to worry about anyone hearing her screaming her head off down the hall. She did wonder for a few minutes if women really did that but decided that she didn't care. This was her night, damn it, and she was going to fucking enjoy every second of it.

Chapter 4

Brad was about as pissed off as he'd ever been. And that was comparing today with a great many other days. Usually, he was about as laid back as a person could be. Not letting anything bother him or just letting things go.

However, today wasn't his day. Nor would it be the person with him if she didn't get her head out of her ass and get away from him. The person sitting at the table with him was human, but he had been around a good deal longer than anyone in the restaurant had been. He'd even hazard a guess that with all their combined ages, he was still older than them. The woman that had sat down at his table while he was waiting on his lunch to be made asked him again if he was going to be much longer.

"As long as I want." She told him that he needed to leave as she was going to be having her meal with her friends here. "I certainly hope there is only going to be one friend—not that I think you have any—because this table only has one more seat than the two you and I are occupying."

"You're going to leave, and we'll have plenty of seating when we move chairs around." He pointed out that all the chairs were connected to the tables, which would make it impossible to move anything. "We'll see about that. I don't know why you took the only empty table in the place in the first place. You look pathic sitting here eating all alone. Go home. Or better yet, walk in front of a truck. You'll make this world a better place for people like me."

"Well, that escalated quickly, didn't it? Not only did you want my table, but now you want me dead. Tell me something, did you just wake up on the wrong side of the bed today, or is this your normal disposition?" She huffed at him. "Yes, well, that's not really an answer, is it? I'm not leaving here until I want to. Which will be when you tire of this bully game that you're thinking you're going to win against me and leave. I have my calendar free for today while you, so you say anyway, have friends coming in to meet you for lunch."

"Oh, you'll see who wins. I'm going to not only get you kicked out, but I'm going to also make sure that I have as many free dinners as I want when I sue this place. I know the owner." Brad just shook his head at the 'I know the owner' claim. He asked her how she was going to manage that. "You'll see."

"You said that already. Not that I care, but you really should come up with a better line. His food was ready, and he didn't want to go up to the bar to pick it up. Knowing that she'd make sure that he wasn't able to sit in his seat again. But the cashier brought him his food and also filled his soda cup for him with sweet tea, his favorite. When Wynonna sat it down in front of him, he winked at her. "Well, I'm starving."

He picked up his meatball sub to take a hardy

bite of it. Just as he was going to sink his teeth into it, the woman sitting with him not only knocked it out of his hands and onto the floor, but she also smashed it with her booted foot. Even his tea that he'd been sipping at was now a part of the décor of the place. All Brad could do was stare at the mess that she'd made with his food, of all things. She was smiling at him like she'd just won some big prize.

"What the hell is wrong with you?" She told him to watch his language. "I will not. You just destroyed my lunch, along with making a huge mess for no reason whatsoever on the floor. Who does that sort of shit? To a fucking stranger. I do hope you know that you're going to—"

"Yes, I know, you're going to try and make me pay for the mess that you made when you didn't consider my feelings. Now that you're finished, you can get out of my seat and be on your way. You know that it wouldn't have come to this had you just done what I wanted you to do in the first place. I've repeatedly told you that I have people coming here to share a table with you, and the fact that you took the only empty seat in the place — "

"It was the only empty seat because the place is busy. Perhaps you should have arrived earlier." She huffed at him, and he looked up at Wynonna at the cash register. "Could you please make me another sub, please? And charge them both to this idiot."

Wynonna came toward him with a roll of paper towels as well as a bucket of what he could only assume was soapy water. It was a mess. Not only had the meal been smashed into the tile, but some of it had ended up on several chairs close to them. A bit of it had even gotten on his boots as well as his suit pants. When Wynonna started cleaning up the mess down on the floor, he took some of the towels and began cleaning up the mess on the table. Sprinkling just enough on the other woman as he went. Petty? Yes, but he wasn't hitting her yet, so that was something.

"I've called the police, Mr. Kirk." Another cashier came to the table and started to clean up the mess that was on another part of the floor. She must have hit it hard to have gotten that far, he thought.

"Mrs. Jacobson, I suggest you either come up with a plausible story to tell them why you'd cause such a scene or get the hell out of here forever. I'm not kidding you right now. I've had enough of your bullshit for a whole lifetime today."

"She's been giving you a hard time too?" Dani, the other cashier, told her how she wanted them to bring in extra chairs so her party would dine. "Yes, she did mention that. I do hope you understand that I didn't provoke this. Correct?"

"Of course we do. She was gunning for some trouble when she walked in. Oh good. The police are here." Dani told the officer where the incident had occurred and how Mrs. Jacobson had knocked the hot sandwich out of Mr. Kirk's hand as she walked them over to the table. "Mr. Kirk was just sitting here reading when she came in and sat down at his table. No doubt trying to pick a fight with him."

"You have it all wrong. I just knew that you were going to make me into the bad guy. When I'm not. Go back to your job before I tell the owner that you've been spreading lies about his best friend."

Everyone looked at him, and all he did was shake his head. "What's the matter with you people? Get out of my restaurant before I have to call him and get him down here for this. It wouldn't surprise me in the least that he fires the lot of you."

"You're sitting with the owner, you big dummy." Mrs. Jacobson turned to the two officers that had come into the restaurant. Then when they shook their heads, she looked at him. "Mr. Kirk owns, operates and runs this place. You thought that you'd get away with saying that you know him? Now that right there is about as funny a thing as I've ever heard today. Makes up for me having to clean up the mess you made too. Hey, everyone. Mrs. Jacobson told Mr. Kirk that she was going to call the owner if he didn't do what she told him to do."

She turned in her seat and looked at him. "You can't be the owner of this place. You're not smart enough to own anything, much less a successful restaurant like this one is." He told her that he not only owned this place but several more businesses that she might frequent. "Sure you do. And I'm the queen of the world. Dumb butt. If that is true, and I'm not saying that it is, you can bet your bottom dollar that I won't be coming in here anymore. This place is crap anyway."

"Of course it is." He turned to the officers that were standing behind Jacobson with their cuffs out and their other hand on their gun. Probably a good idea now that he thought about it. "Now, Officer James, if you were going to ask, yes, I am pressing charges against Mrs. Jacobson. In addition to the insult to my person but also slander, disturbing the peace as well as insulting my staff here by calling them names when she first entered the establishment. I'm sure they'll be more than glad to give you statements about her behavior." Mrs. Jacobson was jerked from her chair and was being read her rights when she looked at him.

"You pansy butt. I'm going to get out in a heartbeat, then I'm going to be coming for you. All you fucking had to do was get up, and everyone would be happy." He didn't miss a beat in telling Officer James that she'd just threatened his life. "No,

I didn't. I promise you when I'm free I'm going to come for you. What do you think is going to happen once they put me behind bars, you big poophead? Nothing. Almost before the door is closed, I'm going to be out. My husband will see to that."

"I would think that he'd want a little bit of 'him time' rather than go and get you out. But that's just me. Having spent the last half hour with you makes me think that you're worse at home than you are out in public." She lunged at him, but it did her little good. The police had her tied up better than he might have done. "When your guests get here, Mrs. Jacobson, what shall I tell them? That you've been hog-tied and arrested, or do you want me to tell them that you've caused enough trouble over the last few hours and will be in jail for a long time? Then remind them that they're next on my list of dumbass women who think that just because they want it, it doesn't necessarily mean that it's theirs."

"You go on ahead and tangle with my friends. That'll be fun for me to think on while I'm waiting on my husband to come and get me out of this trouble.

Go ahead." She turned when someone called her by her first name, he could only assume. "Oh, Porsche, you're not going to believe it. This man here, he assaulted me and hurt me when all I did was ask him if he could hurry his lunch up a little faster as I had very important people coming in. He's trying to tell everyone that he owns this place. Can you believe the balls on this person?" Porsche looked at him.

For just a moment, he could see anger on her face. Then there was recognition. When she put out her hand, he could also see defeat from her. Like she knew that she was entirely in over her head with hanging around with Jacobson.

"Mr. Kirk. I hope you're doing well." He said that he was then thanked her after taking her hand into his. "I don't suppose we can just pretend like none of this happened, could we. My husband is looking forward to the money that your loan will provide for us."

"You've done nothing wrong to be a part of this, Mrs. Brown. However, I might, if I were you, think about certain friendships from now on. While

I don't hold a grudge, I do remember things when they're put before me." She glanced at Jacobson and then back at him. "You might want to, if I were you, have some of your friends have the same idea when it came to hanging out with the wrong crowd, and what will happen should get out of hand as this has today."

"I believe you're right. Not that it matters now, but I was as well as the other girls coming here today to opt-out of being associated with Mrs. Jacobson. I say it that way because she has paperwork on her that she was going to have to have us sign to be her buddies. In crime, I was to understand." He asked her if it was something that the police needed to be made aware of. Again, she looked at Jacobson, who was now screaming at Mrs. Brown that she might well want to rethink not being her friend. She had plenty of money to make her life hell. When she turned back to him, he saw a brilliant smile on her face. "Yes. I do believe that they do need to be made aware of certain things. Thank you, sir. I appreciate you talking to me."

He liked Mr. Brown. David was his first name. His wife, too, for that matter, she had been nice to him when he'd gone to their home to discuss the terms of the agreement to the loan that they wanted to get. A hundred thousand dollars didn't sound like a great deal to most people, it wouldn't even pay for a home in this area, but it would be more than enough for the Browns to get their house finished as well as put a dent, a large one in their credit card debt.

After everyone was gone, Jacobson was still screaming about how she was going to get him. Kirk waited on his sub. He really was hungry. Even though things didn't work out the way he had hoped, he wasn't too terribly upset with how things had gone, either. Some nasty person was going to jail—for now—and he was glad to see that the old bitty wasn't going to harm anyone else with her ways at getting what she wanted. He was glad to see the back side of her when she was taken away.

"Mr. Kirk?" He said that was him and pulled his plate closer to him when the man sat down. "I won't touch your food. Nor will I talk to you as you have been today. I'm Tony Jacobson. I'm here to tell you how profoundly sorry for the trouble that my wife has caused you today. Also, I'm not going to bail her out this time. In fact, I've been planning to leave her since long before this."

"I suggest you get yourself a good attorney." He said he thought that he had one of the best. "Good for you. I'd like to suggest that you change the locks on your house as well. Unless the home is in both of your names? I've heard that recommended to some of the people I know."

"Yes, he's given me a list of things that I should do. That was high on the list, believe it or not. Also, when I called him a few minutes earlier to tell him that she was in jail, he had more to tell me what to do. I'm sorry about you having to have dealt with her. But I'm also very happy that she is in jail for the next unforeseeable future." His food was brought to him, and he asked if he minded him eating. "No. On no, go ahead. I've ordered myself one to take back to the office with me."

Almost as if he'd conjured it up, Tony's sub was

sat in front of him but not made to carry out. When he started to flag down the waitress, Kirk assured him that they could eat together if he wanted. It was nice to have someone calming to eat with after his wife had come into the place.

For the most part, neither of them said all that much. Tony told him that his co-workers couldn't say enough good things about the restaurant, and he'd been impressed when he'd first come for a sub. Now that was all he ate when he didn't have a meeting. They both moaned when they took their first bite. It was Kirk's favorite sandwich when he came into this place. It was one of the main reasons that he'd purchased it.

After they were finished up and their plates taken away, Tony told him about how he'd become friends with the other men with wives that hung out with his. Laughing just a little, he called them the warrior soldiers.

"They make life difficult, I know that. Not just with me and their husbands but, as you already know, with anyone that doesn't give in to their demands when they put them out there. But the one that made me see the light was when I got a call from the high school that our son goes to. He's a senior who is only doing what is required of him to get out of school. I think he believes that once he's out, then he can lay around the house all day with servants waiting on his every whim. He won't, just so you know. You might say that I'm divorcing myself from him as well. Apparently, my wife went there with a gun to make sure that — and this is a quote from her — that no one messed with my son's grades so he'd not be getting into an ivy school. It's not going to happen unless she figures out that she would have to kill off every member of the committee that goes over the records for people. Dan has no more interest in going to college than I do in having to start over in my line of work." They both laughed. "I'm sorry to have told you that. I truly am. I was…it's been a while since I've been able to have a real conversation with someone."

"I know just how you feel. It's been a long while for me as well." Kirk stood up and invited Tony to just take a walk around town. He had something to look into with houses, and he was surprised when he agreed. "My friend from a long time ago has contacted me about some business he's looking into starting. A sort of combination dry-out place along with getting meds for minor things when they needed a place for the people. His wife's father left her enough money to get it done, but they're adding more things into it so that it's a good place for people to get healthy. I believe meals will be served too at some point."

"That's a capital idea. I wanted to start one of those up some years ago for teenage boys. Nothing nefarious or anything but a place for these kids could go for some fatherly advice and such. There are a lot of kids out there that don't have a parent around that can give them just a nudge in the right direction. Plenty of them, I'm thinking." He said that he had thoughts along those lines as well. "Good. I don't know what your plans are for dinner tonight, but the other husband, there are four of us who get together once a week to just not be at home. I think my wife enjoys it when I'm away. I know that I certainly do."

After looking over the buildings he was thinking of selling off, the other men joined them. While Mark told them what had happened in the restaurant, Brad walked into the building that was up for sale too. The little girl pointing a gun at him startled nearly ten years off his life.

"Hello. I'm not going to hurt you." She didn't speak, but he had a feeling that it wasn't that she couldn't but that she didn't trust him to say anything. "I'm thinking of buying this building. I hadn't any idea that you were in here."

"You stand right where you are." He'd moved further into the building, but she wasn't having it. "Me and my sister have been staying here since the dope heads, our parents, decided we was worth more to them dead than alive."

"I'll take care of them if you tell me where they are." Reaching out to the child, he could tell right away that she'd not had a decent meal for a good long time. Then he looked for the sister. "You're sister, she's not well. She's going to have a baby too."

"How the fuck do you know that? And it's

Roger's kid. He raped her." Brad asked her how old she was, knowing that she was just shy of her fourteenth birthday. Her sister, fifteen, was about eight months gone into her pregnancy. "He got to have her because the idiots didn't have enough cash to pay off for the drugs."

He could feel his anger getting the better of him and held onto his temper against the unjust things that had happened to these children. He wanted to help, but he knew too that in order to do that he—

"Hey there, Missy." Tony and one of his friends entered the building. "You don't need that gun, honey. Mr. Kirk here wouldn't harm a hair on your head. Where's Beth?"

"Mr. Jacobson, I don't mind you but is that idiot wife of yours out there? She tried to kill off Beth a week ago when she was walking along the sidewalk. Meaner than a junkyard dog, she is." He said she was in jail. "Good. She needs to stay there."

"Brad, this is Missy Talbot. Her sister is Beth. I've not seen them around in a good long time, to be honest with you, but I'm thinking she could use a good meal and a trip to the doctor." Brad told him about the baby. "Baby? Well, Beth isn't much more than a baby herself. Damned people. Come on over here, Missy and hand me that gun. You know you can trust me."

While Tony convinced Missy to give him the gun, Brad went to the darkest part of the building to find her sister. Beth wasn't sick. She was in labor. More than likely, as weak as she was, it would kill her if she didn't get to a hospital right away. Brad asked Missy if he could call an ambulance for her.

"They'll find us." He promised Missy that he'd make sure they paid for what they'd done to her and Beth. "I've heard that before. The government said that to us and then put us right back with them when they couldn't find no one to take us in. Stupid bunch of bureaucrats."

He called an ambulance after getting permission from the girls. Christ, this was horrific. But the best part was Tony had it all under control, and the girls were well on their way to being well taken care of. He didn't think that they trusted him all that much yet.

"You coming to the hospital with me? I'd feel better if you did." Brad told Tony he'd be there with him. "I'm going to slip over to their parent's house and have a coming to meet Jesus meeting with them. There ain't no cause for this to be happening to those little girls."

"You're going to be going through a nasty divorce here soon, Tony. You'd be better off telling the police what's going on first. I was actually thinking of doing the same, but I know that I'd just be getting myself in trouble." Nodding, the other man entered the first ambulance in the back with Missy. "I'll see you there."

Beth was in a great deal of pain, and it hurt him to see her like this. Just touching his finger to her hand, he could tell that she knew it was from him. Instead of getting all snarky like he figured her sister would have, she asked him what he was.

"Human, for the most part. I had a hand in saving some powerful beings, and they cursed me with this. Not so much as cursed me, but I'm unable to die now. You're not human either." She told him that she wasn't no but a wolf. "Your sister is human."

"Missy is a handful, is what she is. You're right. She's human. Our father is a wolf, and our mother is just a human. They're in trouble with their pack if they find them. We haven't been able to figure that part out just yet." He said that he knew him and if she didn't mind, she'd call him. "Please do. We can't go back there. We'll die if we do." Brad reached out to the only man he'd called a friend since living here.

"I have an issue with something that only you can take care of for me." Donny Kirkbride asked him what he needed. A body disposed of? Perhaps a drinking buddy. *"No, but that might be my second need. I've found the Talbot girls if you're looking for them."*

There was so much tension in the other man's voice when he spoke after a few minutes that Brad could almost feel sorry for the girl's parents. He asked him if they were all right.

"Not particularly. Missy, the younger girl, is totting around a gun bigger than her head, and Beth is pregnant. Apparently, her father didn't have enough for

drugs, so he let him have at Beth. Not my words, but I'm sure you understand. We're headed to the hospital right now." He said he'd send his wife there to be with them. *"If you're going to the house, they're not there. I'm with Beth on the way to the hospital, and she told me that they're staying in the pack barn, holding up there until they can find the girls. I guess you have put out the word that they need to see you."*

"Yes, for a fucking year. They've been...well, to be honest with you, Brad, I've had about enough of all of them fuckers. Growing pot on our land is what got them into trouble in the first place. Is Ben Rogers a part of this?" He told him he was the father of Beth's baby. *"I'll get him too. Anything else I need to know. I'm heading to the barn now. It's full, or I should say that it was full of food we've been using in the harder times of winter. If they touched that, we're going to be hurting by the time spring comes around."*

"I'll help you out with that." He said that he'd appreciate everything that he could do. *"I'll meet your wife at the hospital, then you come there when you have business taken care of. These girls, they're going to*

need a place to live unless you plan on making an example of them too." He said he thought they'd have enough done to them for several lifetimes. *"I'm glad to hear you say that. I'll see you later."*

He told Beth what was going on and that she and her sister were going to be all right. Almost as if they were waiting on them, a large team of people came running out to the ambulance as soon as they pulled up to the front doors.

Tony and Brad waited in the lobby, answering as many questions as they could, glad when Hilda, Donny's wife, showed up with a file to finish up on the questions. He was ready to go home when Beth asked to speak to him about something.

"They were able to stop my labor so that I can go for a bit longer. I don't want my sister out on the streets alone. Can you help her?" It was Donny that answered Beth's question, and he couldn't have been happier with the outcome. "You'll let us go back to the house? I thought we'd be shunned or something."

"No. You're a part of my pack and always will be. We'll help you in any way that we can. First and foremost, the two of you will be staying at my home until we can make better arrangements for your home. Right now, the house, well, it's not fit to be lived in. We may, and I'm leaning toward this better every minute I think of your parents and what they did to the two of you, having it taken down completely and a better, safer house be put on the land." Beth started to cry when her sister was brought into the room with her. "You two will be safe from now on. The pack took care of the four of them."

"Four?" Donny only nodded, and Missy seemed to be all right with that. After being brought up to what was happening, Missy laid her head on her sister's shoulder. "Thank you for helping us. I don't trust you just yet, but so far, you've all been good to your word. Thank you all."

They were both sleeping when he left. There were guards that would be outside their doors until they could both go home. Missy said that she wasn't leaving her sister. She was all she had. It broke his heart to think about what these children had gone through in their short life.

Chapter 5

Warren had never been so nervous as he was right now. He was going to make love to his mate. Not only that, but he was going to bond with her forever. And in a way that he'd never done before. While he knew what occurred during the bonding, he wasn't entirely sure what that would mean for the two of them. How much magic they'd share or if there was more. What would change in them as it had for Hamish and Lander. Warren, musing about silly things that he wouldn't nor could he change, looked up when Robin said his name. The champagne glass that he'd been holding shattered in his hand.

"Do you like…what have you done to yourself?

Damn it, Warren, am I going to have to take you to the hospital? What made you think that you could hold a glass flute in your hand and squeeze it like it was nothing more than a piece of cotton?" Robin took one step toward him when he told her that she was naked. "Well, dud, you dumb ass. I know the state of my undress, thank you very much. Are you hurt badly?"

"No. Not at all." He was healed and smiled at her after showing the wound had disappeared to her. "Christ, you're beautiful. Every part of you is more beautiful than the last."

"Thank you. Is that what had you breaking glass? My goodness, what are you going to do when you have me in your bed? Snarl and treat me like I'm sort of prey?" She looked at him with an impish smile. "Though that does have merit when I think about it."

Warren felt his beast rise up. The need to command, control and to conquer all of her was making him ill with need. However, once he touched his lips to Robins, a calmness moved over him like a cooling waterfall in a lovely setting with just the two of them there. Everything in him paused at that moment like it was regrouping and thinking about what it really wanted to do to his new mate. Warren could hear his heart beating, but it wasn't as fast nor as scary as it had been.

"Are you all right?" He nodded, lifting his head slightly from hers. "You seemed sort of deranged there for a moment. I didn't know what to think. Or is this the usual mode for you? I know so very little about you. And you I. It's sort of sad when you think about it, but we have lifetimes to make memories with each other, don't we, Warren?"

"I love you." He set her away from him, then bent and picked her up from the floor. Holding her like this, like she was something so endearing and comforting to him, he smiled down at her loveliness. "I've never felt this way before. Like I can do anything I set my mind to. Say anything that I want, and it will be all right."

"What is it you want to say? I'm all ears." Even at times like this, where he wanted to make love to her in the worse sort of way, she could easily make him take a step back and find humor in what was going on. "By the way, you can put me down, Warren. I'm sure that I can be a bit heavy holding me like this."

"You weigh nothing at all to me right now." To prove it to her, Warren tossed her up into the air twice, only to catch her again. Robin wrapped her arms around his shoulder and smiled at him. "I could easily get used to seeing this every minute of every day for the rest of my life. I love you so much."

"And I dearly love you, Warren Justice." He put her on the bed gently, even though he was sure she thought he was going to drop her. Without any bounce, he curled his arms around her hips and moved her to the middle of the bed. Letting her legs dangle off the side made his cock stiffen in anticipation and need. It was then that he decided that he didn't want to hurry any of this along and would make love to her for as long as she would allow him to. Forever and a day would suit him just fine.

Putting her legs to the side of the bed, wide apart so that he could have her, he was overwhelmed with the scents that she gave off when he separated her thighs. It was sweet and spicy, strong and bold too. He got down on the floor in front of her and smiled. She was leaning up on her hands facing him with the most wonderfully curious smile on her face that he couldn't read just yet.

"You've no idea how long I've wanted to do this to you." She opened her legs wider, and he felt his eyes roll to the back of his head when her stronger scent rolled over him. "Christ, woman. What am I going to do with you?"

"Give me all that you have." He thought that was the best advice that he could have gotten right then. Sitting up on the floor, moving between her legs, she screamed out what would be the first of many releases when he suckled her clit into his mouth. Nibbling a little, making her juices flow, Warren took as much as he wanted of her into his mouth and swallowed deeply. Her taste, the very nectar of her being, was more than he could have hoped for and then some.

Licking her and drinking her down, Warren

couldn't stop touching her. Even when she begged him to stop and give her a breath, he couldn't. His hands molded her muscles, brought her to him and then away in a way that was like fucking her with his cock. There was so much energy in her cum and scents that he thought that he could never feed again, but like this.

Her thighs tasted of her cream. Her body, hot and sweaty from what he was doing to her, was more than he could have hoped for. When she wrapped her foot around his cock, he nearly cried out at the feeling of it. Christ, his head was going to explode. Suddenly his head was jerked up, and he looked at Robin.

She was beautiful, staring at him with her hair disheveled and hanging in long sweaty strings. It made her no less lovely to see her eyes dilated, her lips swollen like she'd been biting them. Her breasts were pink, her nipples hard peaks. It was all he could do not to go back to what he'd been doing, eating every inch of her and letting her look even more sexy than she was at the moment.

Instead, he got up from the floor to make love to his beautiful mate. Moving around on the bed, he was glad she didn't seem to shy away from his cock. As a large vampire, his cock was thicker and longer than a human, and he was a little nervous about that. When she brushed her hand over his cock for the third time, he took her hand into his and wrapped it around him. Not coming all over her was harder than he thought it should have been, but he loved every second of it.

Touching her with his hands and his mouth was satisfying to them both if her moans of pleasure were any indication. She cried out a couple of times, her body bowing up slightly from the bed when she released. Small ones that seemed to give more than they took from her. Each time she reached for him, Warren moved around so that she could just touch him and not make him come all over her. It was getting harder and harder to do that the more he touched her. As he was moving to her breasts, he felt the need to nip at her nipple and suckle her blood. It was the most powerful thing that he'd ever felt.

Drinking deeply from her breasts was something that he seldom did when he was feeding. Rarely did he feed from women while having sex because it had become boring for him. Had he ever had Robin before any other woman in the world, he thought perhaps he would have perished long ago.

Nipping at her throat while he positioned his cock at her entrance, she looked up at him and smiled. Warren thought that he could go for years, perhaps even decades living off the smile that she gave him. Sliding into her as gently as he could, he was startled when she wrapped her legs around him and engulfed him deeply into her body. Her scream of pain was nearly his undoing.

"I'm so sorry, love." She said she was fine. "No, you're not. You're not fine, and I hurt you." She moved her legs down his, then up again. "You keep that up, and I'm going to believe that you are actually fine and take you right now."

"Take me, please, Warren. I want to be one with you forever." They made love this way, him slowly sidling in and out of her as she touched him.

There wasn't a part of her that was off-limits to him. Nor to her on his body. Each time she dug her nails into his flesh, he felt his inner beast roar up but not in an angry sort of way. Like he was enjoying having her there, making him a part of what was going on.

Warren held her to him as he made love to her. Watching her face make small changes when she was close. It was almost too much for him a couple of times, but he was able to breathe through watching her enjoy herself. And she did. Each time she came, he felt more and more connected to her than ever before.

When she screamed, he stopped moving. Not knowing if he'd hurt her or not, he watched her face as she released. It was magnificent in all her glory. As her body began to harden with her release, Warren nuzzled her neck and bit down hard on her pounding pulse. It was so much more than he'd thought it would be.

Her blood filled his cells. Explosion after explosion seemed to take over his body as he and his beast shared her elixir. Even as he felt his body coming apart, she came again. Her sweet blood continued to fill him and to change him in some ways he didn't understand. Just as he was thinking he couldn't take a second more, his body came apart with the most violent climax he'd ever experienced.

Waking up, he didn't move. Actually, he was terrified to move. Not having any idea what had happened or how he'd ended up in the middle of the bed alone. Reaching out beyond where he was, he could feel Robin in the bathroom. Sitting up caused him to lie back down quickly, and he decided to stay there until she came out to talk to him. It wasn't long before she joined him in the bed again.

Cuddling her body next to his, Warren was happy when she wrapped her body around his. Holding her like this, stroking her back down to the curve of her ass, he asked her how she was feeling. When she didn't answer him right away, he lifted her chin up so that he could see her face.

"I was just thinking of how to put it into words as to how I'm feeling. Overwhelmed? Yes, that's a big one. Sedated? Again, very much so. But there are other feelings that I'm dealing with as well, like the fact that I'm sore. Also, you might not believe this one, but I feel so good. Like I've been given a brand new body, and I'm going to be so much happier in it." She looked up at him. "That sounded silly, didn't it?"

"Not at all. I think that I might be feeling the same way. Like, I've been run over a couple of times but feel better about how it turned out. Like it was the way that I needed to be fixed. Or something like that." He laughed. "Now, *that* was silly. I feel really good. Perfect, as a matter of fact."

They lay there for another hour or so. He knew that she dozed off and on for most of the time. He just marveled at the fact that he was so happy. Not that he'd had a terrible life until then. No more than most vampires had being born in such a time that it was hard to get around.

He thought about that and realized that people, mostly humans, didn't seem to care all that much that there were vampires around anymore. Warren knew that they'd been mostly romanticized in books and movies nowadays. He did often wonder if, at some point, they'd be monsters again. Not that there weren't movies about them becoming beasts of the night and killing all number of people out now, but they weren't as largely seen, he didn't think. Even with the invention of cell phones, where every person in the world had access to a camera and video camera to take pictures and whatnot, he thought it was much easier to get around now. Not that he did all that much in the way of traveling anymore. He told Robin what he was thinking when she asked him.

"I've not seen much of the world. Other than when I could sneak out of the place I was sent to. I don't remember too much of it before I was taken there, but that's all right. Perhaps you and I can make a trip of it someday." He told her he'd love to take her to all the places he'd been. "I bet so much has changed. I know that this little world around me now has a great deal."

As they decided to get up and get going, he realized that he wasn't nearly as tired as he usually was this time of day. Dressing had never been a problem for him, but he did notice that Robin was wearing shorts instead of jeans today.

"My body feels warmer today. I'm not saying I'm cold, I never was that, but I'm almost hot with it today." They headed down to the lower levels, and he was thrilled to see his mother and father there. They asked him if he and Robin had any plans for the rest of the day. "Nothing at all. What did you have in mind?"

Since they were all vampires, they had no reason to go out to dinner or to pretend that was what they were doing when gathered together. However, mom suggested that they go to look at houses. Even though there was plenty of room in their home for them to stay, his mom and dad decided they wanted their own place. A place they could come to at a moment's notice and not have to bother them. He thought it was funny when his mom's face flushed brightly.

"You will be welcome here for as long as you wish. But I'd love to go house hunting with you guys. We can see what the town has to offer in the way of other things too. Not that I have much use for the shops and such, like you, I have been around for a while and have it all, so to speak." He wondered how much she thought a little town like this could offer but was happy for the outing. As soon as they left the house, he was surprised too that he was warmer than normal. Wondering at the change in body temperature, he let it go in favor of hanging out with his family.

~*~

The paperwork she'd been given to go over wasn't working out to the end that she thought it should have. Robin reviewed the numbers several times before simply lying it aside and picking up the next set of contracts. The books that she'd ordered to help her with her job working with Hamish had arrived several hours ago, and she'd yet to be able to open the boxes that they'd come in. Much less see about getting them on the shelves that had been put in for her. She looked up when Lander said her name.

"You looked worried. Or, I don't know,

frustrated. You're very hard to read." She said she was a little of both. Then explained to her about the numbers. "You'll get it. Just step away from it. Come on, we'll tackle these books that you got and put them on the shelves. That way, we can kill two birds with one stone."

"I've never understood that. Two birds with one stone. I mean, I get it, but why the hell would anyone think that you'd be able to kill one bird with a stone, much less two of them. I mean, I suppose it's been done. But really? That's what they came up with?" They both laughed. "When I was still at the start of my punishment with the council, I used to steal books from the library that was close to where I worked. I would return them eventually, but I didn't check them out like everyone else did. Some of the things that were in the older books were just plain stupid and unbelievable." She asked her what part she was speaking about. "Witches. I've known a few of them over my lifetime. Quite a few of them are still around, but the stories that were put out there about them were just stupid. Like the witch hunts of long ago. Who thought up that they could just catch a witch and burn her at a stake? No one could if they were worth anything. A witch of any degree would have been able to cut the ropes they had her tied there with and get away. Written by men, I'm betting. Most of them were now that I think on it."

"I like movies. Mostly to pick them apart. There are times when they'll show a dead body on a coroner's slab that I know is all wrong. You'd think, with all their money and resources, that they'd get that part right. Like bloating and stuff? They never ever look as good as they portray them to be on the set." Robin said she thought it would turn a lot of people off from watching the show. "Perhaps. But my thinking is that if you're going to do it, do it the fuck right. There is so way that a body is going to look like a glamor shot when they've been in the water for a few weeks. Not to mention that their face would be anything other than an indescribable mess. In just a few days, three to five, the body is beginning to bloat, and blood-containing foam begins to leak from the mouth and nose. Get it right, would you please?"

They each talked about their jobs. Robin didn't think that she could have done what Lander did because she was afraid of closed in places. And it couldn't get any more closed in, in her mind, than being underwater. The darkness didn't bother her at all as she had excellent eyesight but not being able to breathe, even though she had no reason to breathe, and it bothered her. Cut off from it, she supposed, is what made her terrified.

Just as they were breaking down the boxes, she realized what she was seeing. Or, in this case, not seeing. Picking up the paperwork, she called for Hamish. He was there in a matter of seconds.

"You said you got this paperwork the day before you met Lander." He said that it had come by special courier. "Her name is on this. All over the place as your partner. I'm not sure what that means in the capacity of this contract, but it basically is dated a day before you met her. It's the dates of her signature, too, that are messed up. Like not just the date but some of them are dated well before she was born. She signed this, or so it says, an entire decade before you even knew that she was around."

Handing him the paperwork, she began to look over the other paperwork that had been given to her. As she read over it, she could see in several places where Lander had supposedly signed the documents that said that all that she had, in the way of monies and land, would be given to the rightful owner at a time when she bonded with Hamish. It took her a while, but she found the source of the trouble just as she was putting the paperwork in the next file.

"My parents did this with the help of the council, of course. They knew that Lander would be coming to you, but they had it set up so that once you bonded with Lander, then you'd be broke. I'm sure that it's more than that, but right now, I'm thinking this is another way for them to have gotten you to do what they wanted." Hamish asked her why they'd do that. "Greed? Power? Perhaps both. But I am going to figure out what my parents had to do with this as quickly as I can. I know you're all this big deal and all, but do you know that you can summon people to you with just their name?"

"I've heard of it. Do you want me to do it now?" She said she wanted to get their paperwork right first. "Good idea. I like that. What will need to be done to make this, so it's not going to happen?"

"The council has already been taken care of, so we have no worries there. Also, and this is a big one, you've bonded with Lander, so there is no threat that came from that, so you're clear there. What I really don't understand is why they thought it would work. I mean, if you're the king of all Vampires, doesn't that sort of trump their ace of taking it all from you?" Hamish explained what he'd been told when they were destroyed. "So they thought they could convince you to just go back to being a lazy poof head and they'd run things the way that they wanted. That explains a great deal that had been happening on my end too. Getting things moved around so that they could find them easily."

"Money, you mean." Nodding, she told Hamish that there is a great deal of that to be held too. Not to mention lands and jewels that had been stored away to be broken down and reused. "Who does it belong to now? I mean, they were taking it from other vampires, correct?"

"Mostly dead lineages. And sadly, there are a great many of those out there, with no one to come forward to claim what would have been rightfully theirs. Also, I'm thinking that a lot of these dead lineages aren't really as dead as the council claimed they were. I've been looking into that as well. I've found a couple of names but not much more than that." He asked her if she had an accounting of all the cash and lands. "More than I think there are numbers for. I'm not joking. Billions upon trillions of dollars all sitting in a cave hidden from everyone, just waiting to be claimed. Why do you ask? You thinking of something to do with it?"

"Help out accidental vampires. Not really accidental ones but ones like you who have been turned away by their family. I'm sure that there are a lot of younger vampires that were turned for no other reason than that it was fun for the sire. Yes, I'm thinking that we can help a great many people with this income. However, I want to make sure that it is a dead lineage before we do that. I'd hate for anyone to come back on us and put up a fuss." She said she'd make sure. "I know you will. I have no doubt that you're not leaving anything to chance at all. If you could do this for me, I think we can make a great many people happier. Or, at the very least, give them enough help to get a start on a new life." Robin told him that she'd work on it first thing tomorrow.

Robin left with Warren, and as they were walking towards one of the homes that his parents had been interested in, Robin realized that the entire town could use a revamping. Things were beginning to look a little out of sorts, run down from what it looked like even twenty years ago, she thought.

Not that she'd spent a great deal of time in this little burg, but she had been looking around recently. Telling Warren what she'd been thinking about, he brought it up to Hamish for information.

As Warren spoke to his parents about it along with Hamish, she wasn't the least bit surprised to hear that Hamish had been thinking the same thing. That the town could use just some sprucing up.

The schools were in good shape and would be for some time, Robin thought. There was a large inground pool for the city to use as well as a nicely maintained playground nearby. As they were walking around, she took note of things like sidewalks that needed to be repaired and roads that needed to have potholes filled in. The library parking lot needed to be redone. She even noticed trees that needed to be trimmed before the winter snow weight brought them down on houses and homes.

Pulling out a small notepad, something that she'd been carrying her entire adult life, she began making notes on the things that he thought would take the least amount of work. Get the little things out of the way before having to resource out the other things. It might make way for a few people to make a few extra bucks come fall when things really started to need to be repaired.

Chapter 6

"Since they're considered non-lethal weapons in most of the United States and Puerto Rico, you can carry them around with you pretty much anyplace you go. And now that you've taken the classes on them, you can feel good about using it too." Rosie picked up her new purchase and liked the weight of it in her hand. She'd not gone for the girly pink or camo but the plain flat black tazer she had been using. "Since the hospital has offered the classes here and you've purchased one, you get a discount to buy other items that you might want to consider carrying around. I heard this is your last day."

"It is. I'm traveling to Ohio over the next month

and then working up there at a larger hospital. I worked there a few years ago." She put the tazer in her backpack and made her way to the elevator while saying goodbye to the officer that had been helping her. "See you around."

More than likely, she'd not. Rosie had been at this hospital as a traveling nurse for the last seven months. There wasn't anything at all she liked here but the very little view she got of the ocean from her camper in the early morning.

She was done with this area. Not only that, but she thought that this particular hospital would be out of business soon the way they did things around here, like the lack of security for their staff. Not to mention, it was in the worse kind of neighborhood for anyplace she'd ever been.

Three nights ago, a group of nurses leaving work had been attacked. Even before that, there had been a man who came into the place through one of the exit doors from the kitchen and stole a lot of meat. The hospital's solution to it never happening again was to tell them they needed to be more careful. Fuck that shit, she thought. I'm out of here at the end of the night.

Getting on the elevator, she was glad that the place had good air conditioning around it. The floor that she'd been working on, Labor and Delivery, had had theirs going off and on for the last few hours. It would be a hot one for women delivering today if she didn't miss her bet. The man that entered the elevator just as the doors were closing had her backing away.

"Where are the babies?" She asked him what he'd said. "The babies. Where do they keep them after they're born? That woman down there wouldn't give me no answers unless I told her a name. I just want to go and see the babies. They calm me."

Alarms went off in her mind. Telling him that L&D was on the fourth floor instead of the second, she pushed the button for four. He asked her where the mommas were then. She said they'd be on the fifth. Not sure what to do now, Rosie pulled her backpack closer around her body and used it as a shield around her front. She only hoped that her lies to the man would give her enough time to be able to warn people of what might be coming their way.

While he was looking at the elevator numbers get larger, she pulled out her tazer and held it in her hand the way she'd been taught. Not having any clue what was going on right now, she just knew that she'd feel better if she was able to protect herself and those babies that were on the second floor if necessary. As soon as the door opened to the fourth floor, the man reached up behind him, pulled out a sawed-off shotgun and brought it forward.

~*~

"You're saying that no one was killed but the woman in the lobby." Douglas nodded, his heart still going about eighty thousand beats a second. "Douglas, if you don't calm the fuck down, you're going to have a massive stroke, and being in this hospital won't even be able to save your ass. One dead isn't the end of the world."

"It is for Ms. James." Well, he was right on that. She had been killed in the line of duty. The lobby receptionist had been killed an hour before anyone found her body. "Did you see all that ammo he had,

Cal? And the notes that he had on him? He meant to kill off every one of them mommas and babies and take him a few nurses and doctors while he was at it. That ain't the brain of a sane man if you ask me."

"I didn't ask you, and you're right. He was off his rocker. But it's done. He's dead, thanks to a quick-thinking doctor, and we're all safe." He said that the woman in question was a nurse. "All right. A nurse. Where is she anyway? I heard that she wasn't doing so well."

"She's doing all right now that they stopped asking her questions. I thought for sure that she was going to cold cock that other officer that was with her. He kept asking her if she knew what he was up to and, if she didn't, why did she tazer him. I think she was thinking out of the box. The one that you tell us about all the time. She sure is mouthy, too, when she's upset. Called my boss a noddle dick. Doesn't sound all that terrible on account of me cleaning it up a bit." He asked again where she was. "Oh. In the nurse's office. Nobody is bothering her right now. She's just sitting in there staring at the machines on the walls."

Cal made his way to the station and asked to see her. The woman at the desk, he thought her name was Connie told him that she'd gone to get her some breakfast and that she'd be back. Shaking his head at the lack of cooperation he was getting from anyone at this hospital was making him glad that he was going to be leaving for Ohio soon. He hated this place.

When she returned, he noticed she made no bones about showing him she was armed. The tazer, he was told, wasn't the one she'd killed the man with but another one that one of his officers had turned over to her. To calm her down, he told him. He'd not met the woman until right now, but she seemed overly calm to him.

"They've held me here long past my time to leave, and I'm starving. If you meant for me to wait on your ass all day, the least you could have done was provide me something to eat and drink. My name is Rosie Thimble. I'm a traveling nurse." When she sat down, opening her bottle of soda and taking a bite of her pastry at the same time, he put out his hand.

"No thanks. I'm not feeling all that generous about my hands being occupied. The man in the elevator, I killed him, correct?"

"The coroner said that he died from blunt force trauma. I'm not sure what you would have done to—" She told him what she'd done. "All right, so that makes sense. How many times do you remember hitting him before he fell."

"Too many. Once he was under me, I stopped. He was a big mother fucker." Cal just nodded. "He meant to kill everyone on the floor, didn't he?"

"Yes. He had a note of sorts. Said that the woman that had given birth to his son had given him up for adoption, and he was pissed off that they'd allow some hoe, his words, to do something like that with his child. You must see a lot of that up there." She told him that she'd never had to kill anyone over it before. "No, I would imagine that you'd not. I'm sorry. I do have a few questions for you that need to be answered."

"I'm not hanging around here. I have things to see to so I can get onto my next job. I killed that man because he pulled out a gun and tried to fire it...he did fire it, but I don't think there was anyone around then." Cal asked Rosie what had made her have her weapon ready. "I can't figure that out yet. I mean, other than what he was asking me, there wasn't too much about him that bothered me."

She looked around the room and stared at the soda machine while she thought about whatever was on her mind. When she'd finished the pastry, he could see that she was a thoughtful woman who didn't talk unless she had plenty to say. And then you'd be well advised to listen to her while she said it too.

"He was overdressed. That's what it was. He had on a hoodie and a skull cap. I could see his face but in shadows. Lower lip had blood on it, too, now that I think about it. Not his, however. I don't know why I know that, but it wasn't. The gun that he had behind his backpack was too high for me to have seen the butt of. he reached for it gracefully, like that was something that he practiced every minute of every day so that he'd not be fucked over when he messed up." Cal started taking notes while she spoke. "The cap was black with an orange design on the front of it. I don't know much about pop culture, so I'd have to say I haven't any idea what that was about. The gloves on his hands were winter ones. Not latex like he might have picked up from here. When he moved to pull the gun out of his back, I could hear the sounds of metal clanking against metal. Like there was a lot, no an enormous amount of weaponry in his pack." She looked at him.

"Nine hundred rounds in his car with other weapons, including knives. Then about three hundred on his person. Along with an assortment of other weapons, including hand grenades. They were named too." She asked him why he'd do that. "I've not read all the notes that he had, but I'm thinking that they were doctors' names that he might well have known had something to do with his baby momma."

She nodded and picked up her trash, leaving the tazer where she'd put it when she'd arrived. Cal asked her about it. Sitting back down after getting herself a bottle of water, she didn't touch it but did stare intently at it while she told him more than he thought anyone else in this hospital knew about her.

"I served eight years in the service before coming out a wounded warrior. I, of course, thought that I was above such things as letting death and carnage get to me, so I spent a lot of my time out fighting a losing battle with my mind. It nearly won. I have a gun. Several, as a matter of fact. One that I carry with me all the time. The one in my bag now is loaded and hot. No one, not a single officer or security officer, asked me about having a weapon. I've been coming in here nightly for the last seven months, and not once have I been stopped with it." She looked at him then. "After I was released from the hospital, I began looking at my life and wondering what the hell I'm doing in it. Nothing that I could see. So I applied for a roaming nurse job, got it and haven't let the daily grind get to me until today. Today wasn't a good day for me."

"I'd say that you're wrong about that. No one was killed other than the lady that wouldn't tell him where the babies were." She said that she'd lied to him about that. "Whatever you did, I'm sure that it's safe to say that you saved a great many lives with your quick thinking."

"I have to go soon. I need to let my dog out. He's more than likely wondering where I am." He asked her if she needed a ride home. "No. I'm capable of taking care of myself."

When she stood up, so did he. He hadn't any idea why but he was going to miss this woman and her ways. In just the few minutes that he'd been with her, he felt a calmness that he'd not felt in some time. Perhaps since before his mate had died some four years ago now. He put out his hand to her.

"I know for a fact that you can handle a gun and shake mine at the same time." She nodded and took his hand into hers. "Thank you for your help tonight. I know you know not to leave unless we tell you to. Also, you might want to see about putting a delay on your departure from here to Ohio anyway. This isn't going to just go away."

"It won't." He saw it then. Just a flash of sadness

on her face. It was profound. Like she was wearing it as a second skin or something close to it. "I'm all right."

"No, you're not. Is there someone that you can call?" She said that she was going to talk to her sister when she got back to the camper she was living in. "All right. I'll come by and see you later today. Rosie, don't do anything stupid out there today, all right?"

She waved him off. For whatever reason, that scared him more than it might have had she had a gun pointed at his face. Ready to tell her that he wanted to stay there until he was ready for her to go, his cell phone went off, and he had to answer it. When he was finished talking to his boss, she was nowhere to be seen.

~*~

Rosie pulled out her service revolver and cell phone and laid them on the little table beside her. She'd tried to take a little nap when she'd gotten home earlier but was too upset to last more than a few minutes at the futile attempt. Joey was laying at her feet right now, soaking up the sunshine and drying his thick fur.

"I think that bear shifter sees more than anyone else. He sure got my number in a hurry." Joey just whined at her. He wasn't much of a talker. "Last time I was able to be that free with my words, it was my sister. What do you suppose she's doing right now?"

Nothing from the peanut gallery. Looking up when she heard something backfire, Rosie put her gun back on the table without even realizing that she'd picked it up again. When it was safe where it was, she went back to thinking about Ruby.

Ruby was her younger sister by four years. Not that she ever acted like she was the younger of the two of them. People had thought they'd been born twins and that they were tight as sisters could be. They were tight, that was for sure, but only because Ruby had a way of calling her up and bashing her for whatever had been in her head. Almost like they were having an out-of-body experience talking to each other, and Ruby would call to get the final word in. She even started the conversations off like that.

No hello, or how are you. But right to the part

where Rosie was either having a shitty day, or she was thinking thoughts that Ruby thought Rosie had no right to. Like ending her life. It had been a real struggle all her life to keep going. It hadn't gotten any better when she'd gotten out of college nor even when she'd enlisted in the service. But last night had been the worse.

Glancing at her phone when it chirped, she let it go to voice mail. It was the cop again. The one that had talked to her when she'd been having her breakfast. Joey stood up and came to her, putting his head on her leg while she petted him.

"I'm all right, boy. That wasn't her." When he seemed satisfied that she was indeed all right, he laid back down at her feet. "I wonder what she'd do if she were here now, Joey? Would she be cursing up a storm or in the camper making me something nastily good for me to eat? I think both. How about you?"

She looked out over the sea of campers and wondered at the ungodly amount of money was sitting in ankle-deep sand and spiders. Not to mention the chairs, flip-flops and towels. The kids, too, were forever leaving their shit either on the walk to the beach or on the beach that ended up around some unsuspecting animal. Shaking her head, Rosie decided that she was going to have better thoughts for the next five minutes.

"Have you seen my doggie?" Rosie shook her head at the woman who lived in the camper not far from where she was. "He's come up missing. Poor old thing. He don't hear well, and I'm afraid one of them sharks come up and got him. Poor old thing."

Rosie didn't know what the elderly woman's story was and usually didn't offer up any kind of ideas about where the dog had gone. If she had been honest with herself, she hadn't ever seen the thing and couldn't have been able to tell anyone if she knew what color it was. Going back to her thinking good thoughts, a group of kids came around the corner of the lane she was in, scattering up sand and shells all over the place. Rosie chose to ignore them. But the man on the other side didn't.

He did this about four times a week when a new group of campers would come into the lot and disturb his vacation. He'd pull out the hose, turn the water on and spray the shit out of the kids. Twice now, the police had been called on him because the water in the hose would get scalding hot and burn the kids. She looked for a lawsuit soon enough, and Rosie was going to sit back and watch it all come about. If she was still here, she told herself. Then she thought about her sister.

They'd grown up in an all-right home. Both their parents had worked full-time. Came home to cook dinner together, then they'd watch a little television and go to bed. If homework wasn't finished up by the time dinner was, dad or mom, or sometimes both of them, would help with that while the kitchen waited until later.

Her phone sounded again, and she resisted the urge to turn it off. It was the cop again, not her sister. If she turned it off and Ruby couldn't get in touch with her, she'd send the police to find her and then make her call her back. It was a game, one that Rosie was getting tired of playing of late.

Their holidays were wonderful. Big dinners

for each of them. A large tree at Christmas time. Vacations to places that most families only read about. Even when they traveled around as she was now, their parents had made a wonderful time of it. They'd have weekend trips too. To places like zoos and amusement parks. Every child's wish and then some.

Then her father had gotten killed. Just a random shooting at a convenience store that not only cost his life but that of four others in the building. Mom took it hard, and they had to move in with her parents. Life took an abrupt change on that night, and she and her sister never had a good child life after that.

"Of course, I was seventeen by then and should have figured out my life before that. I mean, it was too good for too long, don't you think?" Joey huffed at her, something that he did on occasion. "You know the stories. I couldn't get my head out of my ass to save my life, and it cost me. And my mother."

Mom had committed suicide just after Ruby had turned eighteen. The note that she left them said that she didn't want to be around any longer and wanted to be with their dad. He had been and would always be her world. That hit them both hard, having thought that they were their world when they were growing up. Rosie's life took a tumble, and it had been almost too late for her to get back on the right path toward the end of it.

This time when her phone rang, Ruby's face appeared. Picking up the phone, she was sobbing before she could even say hello. It took her a few minutes to realize what her sister was saying to her when she was able to calm down.

"I said where are you? I'm here in this god-awful park you're in, and I don't know where to find you." She told her the lot number she was in. "Good, not too far from me. What are you doing not at work? I thought you had another week to go."

Just as she was about to tell her what had happened and the date today, she saw her sister pull into the place next to her camper. Rushing to her, nearly tripping over Joey to get to her, the two of them hugged and talked all over each other until they had to sit down. Joey was excited to see Ruby as she was, and they bonded while she sat there looking at the two of them.

"I had a feeling that you were in trouble. Then early this morning, I had a feeling that you needed me. I don't know what prompted me to come to this place, other than it's cheap and run down, but I found you. I'm going to stay with you for a while if that's all right with you two." She asked her sister what was wrong. "Always right to the point, aren't you? I'm dying. I have a brain tumor about the size of a golf ball that can't be operated on."

She was stunned to silence. Her thoughts on ending her life circled around in her head as she sat there. And now her sister was going to die through no fault of her own. Not sure what she could say to her baby sister, she sat there while she talked to Joey and told him what a good dog he was being.

"When did you find out?" She told her a few days ago. She'd been having a lot of blackouts and went to see the doctor. "I hope you saw a specialist. Someone other than just a doctor. I'm not saying that they're not right. But a second opinion wouldn't hurt."

"I've seen several specialists. Not to mention surgeons, as well as anything else that I had hoped to get better news from. All of them say the same thing. The tumor has advanced to the point where it's too large and set in to be taken out without leaving me with nothing more than just a dead brain." She nearly said that she would take that but didn't. But losing her sister was more than she could think of right now.

"I know someone." She asked her if he was a miracle worker. "He might be. He's the responding officer to the trouble at the hospital. Not that he was a cop but a physicist that was...never mind. That's not what is important. He's a shifter. You can be healed if you allow him to change you." Her sister was already shaking her head. "No, don't do that. I can't lose you, Ruby. You're all I have in the world, and you keep me balanced."

Picking up her phone, she made the call to the doctor who had left her several messages. Not bothering with looking at them, she redialed his number and talked to Ruby. Things had to be better for her sister. If for no other reason than that she —

"You're a very difficult woman to get in touch with." She told him where she was and that he had to come to her right now. "Are you all right? Did something happen?"

"No. I mean, yes. Just come here. My sister is here, and I'd like for you to meet her. I need something from you to save her life." The silence was very telling, and she started to cry. "You can turn me down when you get here. But right now, I need for you to come and talk with her so that you can see if you can help her. She's all I have in the world right now, and I can't lose her. You have to come."

As they waited for him to come to them, Rosie ordered pizza. It was a good place to get food from, and they delivered. While she was taking care of that, Ruby went into her camper and started fussing at her about how messy it was.

It really was. But she'd been working so much to get this job under her belt that she didn't care. Now she could see that it was much she'd left things to go. Even having a washer and dryer in the place, she'd not done any laundry other than what had to be done. Helping her clean up things, she was glad now that she was going to have clean sheets on her bed for the two of them. Tonight, they'd talk. Then tomorrow, there would be actions taken. As soon as the knock sounded at the door, Rosie let out a long breath and opened the door.

"Come in." As soon as he was in the trailer, Cal just looked around. "Ruby has gone to get some sodas for us. I wasn't sure what you might be wanting to drink, so there are beers in the fridge."

"Water is fine." Cal looked around again. "I don't know what you think I can do for you and your sister, Rosie. I mean, I'm just a bear shifter that hasn't had a great deal of luck in life. I can help her, but that might only be extending her life. And not in a good way."

"Give us time. That's all I ask for. She's all I have." He nodded and then finally sat down. When her sister came back, she helped her bring in the sodas and other things that she'd not known she was out of. Cal helped with the bags, but when they were all standing in the kitchen of her camper, he just stood there holding onto the last two bags of groceries that he'd brought in.

"This is Ruby, my sister. She's dying. I need you to fix her for me." He didn't stop staring at Ruby. "Are you all right? Say something."

"You're my mate." Ruby told him what she'd been saying all along, that she didn't have long to live. "You will now. I mean, my blood will heal you completely. Or at least until such time as I can change you. If that's what you want."

"I don't know you." He said that he didn't know her either but didn't want her to die either. "I don't know. This is all strange to me. I mean, we both know a lot of shifters, but none that...why are you really doing this? Do you think that it's going to be easy on you or something to have a mate around?"

He burst out laughing. And Rosie had a feeling that he was just as startled by the sound as they were. When he finally handed over the bags, he sat down. He made no effort to touch her sister, but he did stare at her.

"I'm a very old bear shifter, Ruby. I've been around…Christ, longer than a lot of vampires I know. That's where I was going. Am going. Tomorrow. I have a friend that is opening up a clinic where I'm going to be working at. Sort of get away from…I had a mate once. She died some time ago in childbirth. It happens sometimes but not often anymore. But I lost them both. I thought that I was going to be alone for the rest of my life and going to see Hamish, it would have—"

"Hamish Perry?" They both turned to look at her. "His name is Hamish Perry, isn't it? He contacted me through the travel board to come and help out with the clinic that he's opening for men and women to get help. Not just dried out, but—he's a vampire? Well, ain't that funny? Not really, but…we'll leave in the morning. The four of us. We'll eat now and then pack up to go."

"Wait, it's not that easy. I'm in the middle of an investigation. And so are you." She told him that she was leaving and he'd better make up his mind to go with them, or she'd hurt him. "You're really that bad assed aren't you? All right. Let me make a few calls. And then talk to Hamish. How did you know that it was him?"

"How many people do you know that have the first name of Hamish?" Rosie was so happy that they both laughed. And when their dinner arrived, she was glad that she'd ordered a meat lovers for Joey. He was her best bud, and she loved the guy.

That night she discovered that her sister had already sold off her home and had gotten rid of all the things that she had. Whatever she couldn't sell had been donated, and they were well on their way to getting to Ohio.

Cal was going to have to work in the morning on transferring the information that he had, and she and her sister were going to get a start on packing up the camper. With being in one place for these last few months, she'd forgotten how long it took to break things down when she was ready to go. Rosie had gotten used to having her things out where she wanted them and was now regretting that decision.

But she also knew that as soon as she was settled in Ohio, the same thing would happen, and she'd have to bitch at herself for letting things get so lax.

At midnight the two of them were in bed. Since it had been so late talking, Cal had decided to stay in the spare bedroom at the end of the camper. She and Ruby ended up falling asleep, holding each other and crying for most of the night. It wasn't what she wanted, but Ruby was going to be all right, and she'd have her around for a bit longer. It was going to be all good.

By six-thirty, they were ready to go. Pulling out with Ruby behind her in her rental, she followed her to the rental place. By nine, they were on the road and having a good time. Rosie was glad for this time with her sister and was happy too when Cal decided that he'd take his truck home and meet them there. It was hard on the man, she could tell, but he seemed to understand that this was something that the two of them needed. And she did. More than she would have thought possible.

Chapter 7

Warren felt his body being turned inside out. From the inside of his toes to the top of his head, a roar like that of a great beast rolled through his body and out of his mouth. It both hurt and felt amazing. Whatever was happening to him, he wanted it to both stop and go on forever if it didn't die from it first.

Dizzy with these feelings, it took his befuddled mind several seconds to realize that he'd just had a powerful climax and that his body was trying its best to recoup while his mate continued to fondle and lick his shaft. Pulling Robin up from his waist where she'd been sucking his cock while he slept, he held her. She wasn't happy that he'd come before she'd had her fun, apparently.

"I'm not finished with you yet." He said he didn't think he could move. "Too bad. I'm going to get my fun, and you're going to give it to me."

When she sat on his hardening cock, he watched her. She was so beautiful when she was riding his cock. She'd been doing it a lot more lately, waking him from a sound sleep so that she could take her pleasure. While she never left him hanging, right now, he wasn't sure that he could do much more than watch her as she rode him.

"This is the best part of having morning sex with you." He asked her what she meant. "You're satisfied for the moment and not trying to rush me into you coming with me. And your cock fills me as you get hard again. Like you are now."

It was difficult to watch her pleasure herself and not get hard. He might not be able to come again, he was simply empty, but he could enjoy giving her pleasure. The more noises that she made, her scent perfuming the air around them, he did indeed get hard. Rolling her to her back, he suckled at her breast and throat. Fucked her until she begged for more, then would stop. Each time that she was close, he teased her more. This was the game that they played each and every morning, and he could find no reason to change up things now. Christ, she was going to make him dead just as much as if he'd met the sun.

Her body responded to his like he loved. Each time he touched her in a place, he would go back and nip at the flesh there. She would be covered in little bites when they showered, but they healed quickly. When he got to her throat, a place that he so loved to feed from her, she moved her neck in a way that gave him her all.

"This is where I want to be most of the time. Right here, with you sucking at my throat, feeding you." Warren said that he loved her. "And I love you so much."

His cock moved in and out of her over and over. Warren could feel his balls fill, his cock swell with the need to empty. But he continued to tease and play with her until they were both ready.

He licked along her ribs. Suckled more at her breasts. Warren even licked along her arms to her shoulders and nipped at her there. Her ears were laved, and he tasted her hands. Making love to all of her, touching every inch of her, Warren felt empowered and in love.

"Please? I need more." Warren wanted Robin to have it all. And more. But he wanted her completely sated too. She was his world, and he wanted everything to be perfect for the two of them. Making love to her was the only way that he could think of to show her just the full meaning of being in love with her.

When she was beneath him again, Warren held her hands in his above her head. While he made love to her, telling her of his need and love, he never stopped touching her. Her skin was like a warm blanket. Her body was his. Even as he tried to let her body come with his, he knew in his heart that she would never be anything but his first priority in all things of life.

Her face was beautiful when she came. Her

body softened by degrees as she released. It was an amazing thing for him to watch. Her body building up to something so powerful and so lamely called a release that he wanted to find a word that would be better.

The softening of her face as she came for him. Her body relaxing into a soft mound. Lashes as long as his fingernail laid out on her cheeks. Lips, swollen from his own administration, curved up into a smile that he felt all the way to his toes.

Soft breath blew over his own. Her scent was like fresh fruit and clouds as he tasted it from her. As she held onto her conscience, just for a few seconds, Warren knew that she was as good as sleep as he was going to be in a few minutes.

"I love you dearly, my heart." She smiled, a small smile that made him grin. "You are my everything and will be forever. Sleep, my love."

Warren watched her for over three hours. She never moved around in the bed in all that time, nor did he. Just watching for the moment that she opened her eyes because he wanted to be the first person that she saw when she did. But duty called him, and he had to meet Hamish at one of the houses that he was hoping to purchase.

"You're looking all sappyish." Warren could only grin at his friend. "Yes, having a mate can make you do and say things you would never have thought of doing before. Don't you think so?"

"She's like my heart and my soul all at one time." Hamish would and did understand what he was talking about. "All right. What are we doing out here for this building? I assume you have a reason for pulling me from my bed so early in the evening."

"I need to have it cleaned out so that I can have a crew come in and do the evaluation." Warren asked him what he was talking about. "The building needs to be inspected, but I can't get anyone to go into it because of its occupants. There are a great many of them hiding in the building that needs to be shooed out."

"Shooed out? What the fuck are you talking about? Great many what?" Hamish just smiled at him. "This isn't getting us...oh no. Oh no, you're not talking about fucking faeries, are you? I hate faeries. They're annoying as fuck, and they're tiny."

"You hate them because they're tiny? That's the dumbest reason I've ever heard. How can you hate something because they're smaller than you." He told him that he was afraid of stepping on them or something. "So you hate them? Warren, they're just little things. All I need for you to do is go in with me so that I can tell them that they can't stay in the house any longer and that it needs to have humans living there."

"How come you didn't bring Lander to do this?" He told him why. That made Warren laugh. "Yes, she'd want to keep them all. And have them living in your house. I can see her doing that. I can. But I'm not going to go in there first. They'll be… they'll be all over me or something, and I can't stand that."

"Just help me out." As soon as the two of them entered, he knew that this was going to end badly. Not only did they swarm Hamish as the new king of vampires, but they had to congratulate him as well.

They were all over him, like attaching themselves to his hair and clothing. "Enough."

Once they were across the room, he was able to get himself under some control. Looking around the room, he was startled by the sheer number of them living in the place. Thousands upon thousands of them were living in the small space so deep with them that he knew that it had to be difficult to move for them.

It took the two of them nearly four hours to get things sorted out. The person that was in charge of the region where they were living had run off. Whatever that meant, and they'd not had anyone to report to. Again, he had no idea why that was important to their duties, but that was what they'd found out. After Lander and Robin came to help out, they were stuck with the task of not just finding them better housing and more of it. But they also needed to have jobs. Keeping them busy would keep them out of trouble.

Some of them were sent to another region to help out with the fall. It really wasn't something that they could have done, they weren't in charge of the little people, but they were so grateful for having someone helping them that they did just what they were told. Robin had a lot of information on the faeries and helped in being able to find the right food and homes for them to live in too.

"I've sent a group of them to the river's edge to make sure that the fishing lines are all cut so that they don't trap any little ones. They're dangerous for the smaller faeries, so having them removed will keep injuries down as well. While they're doing that, a few of them will start on homes for the families that need them." Lander asked if they would be all right there in the winter months. "No. We'll need to find them housing or a place like a greenhouse to live in before then. Also, I don't know if you're aware of this or not, but they'll need to belong to someone before too much longer. By belong, I mean having someone to rule them. Once there is someone in place that is in charge, they will work better together too. I haven't any idea why that is, but that's what I know about them."

With her knowledge, not only did Robin have the number of them dwindled in numbers, but she also had some of them set up a clinic for themselves and a few places where they could get fresh water. Lander had told them where they could find water reeds that they could use for roofs. Even Hamish's grandda brought over some small blocks of wood for them to use as well as some tacks and such.

By the time they were ready to call it a day, the building they had gone to empty was still occupied but not by as many faeries as before. Some of them were only resting the night there before traveling to the next area, and others were working on getting the things they'd been given sorted out for the others. Tomorrow he was going to go with Hamish to pick up more blocks of wood and crayons for them to use as well as glue. It was his idea to help them with the colors for their new homes.

"I've never seen the like." Charles patted him on the back as they were headed back to the house. "I wonder where their queen is if she's just letting them fend for themselves. Something might have happened to her or something."

"I guess there would be a queen of faeries. I never gave it much thought. Do you suppose that Robin might know how to get in contact with her?"

"Don't know why not. She's a smart little cookie. Smarter than I think she realizes she is." Warren agreed with him on that. Robin was good at second and even third guessing herself when she was working. Or even talking. "You get that girl to look into things, and I'm betting that in a couple of hours, she'll not only have the information on the faerie queen, but she'll also know what to do with the rest of those little people. You know they'll be safe with her around, too, don't you?"

"I do. She's been watching over them since she got here. Told me that they're the reason for everything. I've never really thought of that before, but I think she might be right." He smiled at his old friend. "I'll talk to her when I get back. She's gone to the store with Lander to pick up some supplies that the clinic will need. It's hard for me to imagine that a little bag of cotton balls could be used for so many things once they're used on little people."

They talked about makeup pads and cotton swaps and the million and one things that they were being used for. There were also the crayons that he knew she was to pick up too. The colors would be beautiful on the walls and could cheer up even the sickest patients.

"Mirror. Be darned if I never thought of a mirror being used for so much. I have to admit to you that I durn near burst my gullet when that little fella told me that he wanted to use them for the ceiling in his bathroom. That way, he'd not miss any parts of himself when cleaning up." They both laughed about that. "I'm going to go and see if I can find some scraps of material for them too. I'm to understand that they can use that for just about anything too. But mostly blankets and such."

They had a list, the five of them. Robin had pointed out that if they each had something they were looking for, they'd not have too much of any one thing. Also, he was going to see about having more flowers planted in the downtown area. He'd heard them talking and said they don't go there to see the flowers anymore because there isn't enough drinking water. The downtown area in this little town really did need a bit of cleaning up. He was going to see to that himself when he got up in the morning.

The rest of his evening was spent walking around with Charles. They found plenty of things along the way for them to pick up to take back with them too. He'd found a wooden basket that had fallen out of a trash can and taken it with them to fill. By the time they were at the house again, he'd been able to nearly fill it to the top with things that he'd picked up. A broken soda bottle — the glass would be good for making things pretty, he'd been told. A few bottle capes that could be used for chair tops. The list of reusable things was as long as the list to use them for, he thought. And all from just walking around the town.

"I'm going to start doing this more often. Take a faerie or two with me to help me decide if I'm picking up crap or not." Charles said they'd enjoy that too.

Warren put it on his list of things to do, starting after tomorrow when the Hardbottoms were summoned. "I do hope that goes well. Don't you?"

"It will. They'll get their comeuppance, and the world will be a better place." Warren hoped so. If for no one's place but his Robins. She was more worried than anyone that something was going to go wrong.

~*~

Robin had it all handled. Looking around the big room, she was afraid she'd forgotten something. Some small detail that was going to have her messing up her future along with the people that she'd come to love so much. Hamish and Lander included. When Charles, Hamish's grandda came into the room, he took the file from her and put it on the desk. After showing her to a seat, he sat down beside her in the next chair.

"You're going to have to take a breath, my dear, or this will never get done. Breathe in and out, and you'll be fine." She told him where her thoughts were. "Yes, I can see where you'd think that. But you've also been going over this in your mind and office since it started. It's all going to come out well. If not, then my grandson can just end them, and that will be the end of the trouble. Don't you think? Well, I'm thinking that they need it anyway, but then I've never been one to hold out much hope that someone will be able to change their ways after being so bad at it for so long."

"I might well agree with you. They've been terrible people since before they met each other. The saying that the fates make a match is true. There couldn't be two people more matched at being hateful and evil than the two of them. Then there are my sister and brother. Christ, it's small wonder they, too, haven't been brought up before any kind of board." He asked her how many times her parents had been. "Not nearly as much as they should have. They were in the pockets of every council that has been formed. I'm talking not just vampires but also bears and cats too. I've contacted their kings as well. They're going to get whatever is left from Hamish."

"Does Hamish know about all this other stuff?" She said that she'd gone over everything with him last night. "Yes, well, knowing you like I do, I'd say you've gone over with him more than just last night. And have given him notes to go over as well."

"I have. I don't want this to come back and hurt any of them. I've grown very fond of them all. Including you." He patted her on the leg and told her that he loved her as much as he did the others as well. "Thank you. I know that as king, he can pretty much dictate what happens to all of us when we come up before him. But I don't want people, other vampires, to be afraid to come forth when they have trouble, but I also want them to respect his word too. That he is going to do just what he says he is when he says it. It's been a very long time since anyone has felt like they could go to someone about issues that are going on within the organization."

"I would hazard a guess that you've got every one of them written down for him too." She felt her face heat up in embarrassment. "Just as I thought. Well now. We're all here. Hamish is in the kitchen preparing the household for his friend Calhoun coming. Also, a couple of young women have joined him as well. Don't know a great deal about them, but I'm to understand that one of them is very ill."

"I've spoken to Calhoun Meyer a few times. He's coming here to work with me in the clinic. Also, I do believe that one of the women coming is a sister to a traveling nurse that we've hired. She's supposed to be extremely good at getting to the heart of a problem." She wondered just for a moment if she should mention the incident that had occurred in the hospital before they left, but apparently, Charles had already heard about it. "Yes. She saved a great many people. Seemed sort of pissed off about it, too, from what I heard. Her name is Rosie. Her sister, the one that is very ill, is Ruby."

"It's time." They all gathered in the living room that had been stripped of all the furniture and hangings on the walls. She had asked for the things to be moved out in the event that things got hairy, and she didn't want any of the household hurt from it. The people would be safe as she could make them, and since this was going to be a trial of sorts since everyone knew they were guilty already, she wanted nothing for her family to hide behind when it came time to end them. If that was what Hamish and Lander decided to do.

She loved how they worked so well together. It almost seemed as if they'd been working like a team since well before either of them met. Lander was always the level-headed one. Cool under pressure. If she was quietly thinking, it was because she was going through many options to see if they worked before she said what she wanted to do. Hamish was somewhat like that, but he was a good deal more vocal about his ideas.

He'd toss them out as he rejected them. Telling anyone around him why he had decided that it would work and would move on to the next idea. She did wonder at times if he did the same thing when he was alone. Just bullet-shooting random thoughts until he got to the one he was going to use. It would be like him to do that. The man was the nicest person she knew but also the oddest.

"How much do you have for me? I mean, other than their names?" Robin explained to Hamish what

she had in the way of names as well as how he had
to say the entire thing she'd written out of him. "Yes.
You said that these are their original names, and any
other aliases will automatically be known afterward.
The list will fill in here for us to take action on."

"Not us. You. I've gone over that with you.
Right?" He asked for a reminder. "All right. I or
Warren can summon them here as yours and Lander's
seconds. But we cannot compel them to speak. If
you summon them, which you are, then you have
complete control over them. They will only do what
you say when you tell them to do it."

"Why is that so important?" She told him. "Yes.
I want them to tell me the truth. But they don't have
to with you."

"They don't have to, no. I have a feeling that
they're going to try and lie to you as well, but in this,
we can make it work out for a great many people." He
knew all this, but he, like her, was nervous. This had
to work. Without it working out for the people, her
parents, then others would see that he was a failure,
and that would be bad for him. "Hamish, thank you

for allowing me to help you with this."

"I wanted to talk to you about this anyway. They're going to die. All of them are. You're aware of that, I know, but I'm going to be killing your parents." She said she knew that. "No. I know in your head that you know that, but I want to make sure that you're heart is all right with it as well. To make sure that this never comes between us. I don't know that I could go through with this, thinking that it might someday hurt our friendship."

"Hamish, don't worry about what effect them being dead will do to me. As far as I'm concerned, they've been dead for a long time before this. I had washed my hands of them so long ago that I'm not entirely sure that I could pick them out of a crowd if need be. I have more information on them now, today, than I did long ago. They're nothing to me. They left me there long ago. Decades and decades passed without contact or word to me. The day they did that, Hamish, I never thought of them again as my family." He told her that they'd be dead. "They, more than anyone that I know, deserve it." Then she asked him if he was ready.

"I am." After she handed him the slip of paper with the names on it, he read it over several times before he nodded at her. "They'll be bound as soon as they enter the room, right?"

"If you do this right. Yes." Hamish laughed, and she turned in the room. Nothing was going to mess this up. She'd worked much too hard for it. When Warren joined her, they turned to the doorways and waited.

"Sherman Alvin Hardbottom and any other name you have used or been called since, Cybil Susan Waldwick Hardbottom and any other name you have used or been called since—" He not only named her brother but her sister as well in the names to be brought forward. Even though her sister was 'supposed' to be dead, it was difficult to know for sure until she didn't show up. But her parents and brother were there, bound to the floor by silver chains and magic. Her mother, as usual, was the first person to be pissed off.

"What the hell is the meaning of this?" She told

Hamish to let her go. "You've no right to summon me like I'm nothing more than a...dog on a leash or something. What do you think is going to happen when the council finds out what you've done? They'll behead you. That's what will happen."

"I'm not worried about them or you. I've called you here to have a conversation about the things that I've found out that you and your little family here have done." Cybil asked him again who he was. "Hamish Perry. I'm the king of the vampires. This is my mate, Lander. Also, my seconds, Warren and Robin. Does that satisfy your questions?"

"Where is the council? They said they had this under control when I spoke to them last. They were going to make sure that you knew the rules." Hamish explained that he knew the rules very well, thanks to her. "Well, I'll be the judge of that. I want them here now. David, Scott and Amy. I want to speak to them." No one moved to do her bidding. "Did you hear me? I said to bring them here. I'll get to the bottom of this right now."

Sherman, her father, tried to pull his mate back.

While she was still on the floor in silver, she was just able to inch her way toward Hamish in what could only be considered an aggressive way. It was Warren who stopped her progress by stepping in front of her before she could touch the new king.

"Cybil, honey, I think we should come back at another time." Hamish informed her father that there would be no other time. "Please. You can't do this to us. We're an old family. We shouldn't be having the kind of fun like we used to. I know that now. But we'll—I have a daughter. She's worthless if you have taken care of the council. I don't know what she ever did for them, but she wasn't worth the spit it took to make her. You can have her for our fines. I'm sure that as my daughter, she's got to be worth something. Right?"

"I'm his mate's second." Her father looked at her while her mother screamed about being let go and to also bring the council members to her so that she could get this straightened out. "My mate, Warren Justice, has found many uses for me, father dear, and we have been promoted to being the seconds to the king and queen of all vampires."

"No. No, I won't believe that. You were of no value then, and you are no value now." Hamish asked him if he thought to give him a worthless vampire. "Like it matters. You'll just have to — surely it was explained to you that we're in charge of the vampires and their money claims. It's been done this way forever, and it won't stop now that you've gotten some kind of — we'll just have to take care of you the same as we did that other man. I don't remember his name right now, but they can — you destroyed them. Damn it, man. Have you any idea how long we had to work to get them to do what we wanted? Now we're going to have to start again. What right did you have to interfere with our work?"

"Every right. As I said, I'm the king of all vampires." Her father, or whatever he was to her, just waved him off. "You think that you're above the laws that govern us?"

"Well, of course, I'm above them, you idiot. Oh, Cybil, do shut up." Mother's mouth closed like it had been hinged. "Your caterwauling is giving me a pain in the head. This man, he's messed things up for us, and this upstart here is claiming to be our child. See if you can talk some sense into her so that she'll let us go. Then I'm going to have to start all over with someone to do as their told. Christ, why couldn't you have just been like the other man? Lazy. Have you any idea the amount of work that I'm going to have to do now that you've been making changes to our work. Plenty. I can tell you that."

Hamish looked at her while her father was going on and on about what he had to do. At one point, she watched as he sat on the floor, yelling at her mother to make notes. That was when Robin noticed that her brother wasn't speaking. He only lay there on the floor with the chains draining his life, staring at her.

"You're not ugly at all." Robin let go of a little burst of laughter and asked him why he'd say that. "I remember you being short and fat. I guess I didn't look at you for a long time. Not that it matters, you are going to do as father says. He'll never like you as much as he does me now that Jamie is gone. I had to kill her, you know."

"Why is that?" He explained what she'd been doing behind his back and that had pissed him off. "So she was trying to bring up a case against the three of you, and you decided that her being dead was better for you all. Sounds like another crime against the family if you were all in on it."

"Of course we were. Not only that, sister dear, but as our family, you are required by blood to save us. Don't you know that rule? You're not going to be able to kill us because it's written that you can't kill family. We're your family, much to my shame." She laughed, knowing something that her brother didn't. Like she's not the one going to wield the magic, but Hamish is. "Your mate can't do it either because he's family now. Doesn't that just suck for you? I think that I'm going to love having you as the second to the king. This might work out better for them than I thought it would. You are going to be doing all kinds of favors for me that are going to make me the richest vampire in the entire world. And you can't do shit about it."

He looked at her, pouting, then started laughing. She joined him. Instead of reaching for the sword to take off their heads, she watched her brother's face as Hamish did so.

It took less than a second for the sword to come across her father's neck. Once he was gone, not even dust in the room, Hamish turned to her mother and ended her life as well. Before Hamish could kill her brother, she stooped to his level and smiled at him. Watching his face as his head was removed from his body was something that she had never hoped to see. His life ended quickly and without much fanfare.

"Are you all right?" The furniture had been put back, and the office cleaned up. Warren came out to sit on the deck with her. "Hamish has a group going to the house they were hiding in to get the things that were left behind. There is some talk that the place has a lot of baby vamps in it that were doing their bidding. Hamish is afraid that they're wild and might need to be put down because of their treatment."

"They will be. I only found out about them this morning. Hamish has their information on hand." He pulled her up from her seat and put her on his lap. "I need a vacation. How about we do something before Hamish gets too busy with running the vampires."

"I'd like that myself. You tell me where it is you want to go, and we'll go. I'll talk to Hamish about it. I'm sure he'll agree with all you've done for him over the last few days." She said that if he didn't, then she'd hurt him. "I do believe that you would too. I love you, Robin Justice."

"And I love you, Warren Justice."

Before You Go...

HELP AN AUTHOR

write a review

THANK YOU!

Share your voice and help guide other readers to these wonderful books. Even if it's only a line or two, your reviews help readers discover the author's books so they can continue creating stories that you'll love. Log in to your favorite retailer and leave a review. Thank you.

AWARD WINNING, BESTSELLING AUTHOR

Kathi Barton, a winner of the Pinnacle Book Achievement Award and a best-selling author on Amazon and All Romance books, lives in Nashport, Ohio, with her husband, Paul. When not creating new worlds and romance, Kathi and her husband enjoy camping and going to auctions. She can also be seen at county fairs with her husband, who is an artist and potter.

Her muse, a cross between Jimmy Stewart and Hugh Jackman, brings her stories to life for her readers in a way that has them coming back time and again for more. Her favorite genre is paranormal romance, with a great deal of spice. You can visit Kathi on line and drop her an email if you'd like. She loves hearing from her fans. aaronskiss@gmail.com.

Follow Kathi on her blog: http://kathisbartonauthor.blogspot. com/

www.ingramcontent.com/pod-product-compliance
Lightning Source LLC
Chambersburg PA
CBHW020620180626
46810CB00007B/2872